One Real
Thing

P9-DFK-228

clearwater crossing

One Real Thing

laura peyton roberts

BANTAM BOOKS
NEW YORK • TORONTO • LONDON • SYDNEY • AUCKLAND

RL 5.8, age 12 and up
ONE REAL THING
A Bantam Book / April 1999

All scripture quotations, unless otherwise indicated, are taken from
the HOLY BIBLE, NEW INTERNATIONAL VERSION®. NIV®.
Copyright © 1973, 1978, 1984 by International Bible Society. Used by
permission of Zondervan Publishing House. All rights reserved.

All rights reserved.
Copyright © 1999 by Laura Peyton Roberts.
Cover photography by Michael Segal.
Cover art copyright © 1999 by Bantam Doubleday Dell
Books for Young Readers.
No part of this book may be reproduced or transmitted
in any form or by any means, electronic or mechanical,
including photocopying, recording, or by any information
storage and retrieval system, without permission in
writing from the publisher.

If you purchased this book without a cover you should be aware
that this book is stolen property. It was reported as "unsold and
destroyed" to the publisher, and neither the author nor the publisher has received any payment for this "stripped book."

ISBN 0-553-49257-8

Published simultaneously in the United States and Canada.

Bantam Books are published by Bantam Books, a division of Random
House, Inc. Its trademark, consisting of the words "Bantam Books" and
the portrayal of a rooster, is Registered in U.S. Patent and Trademark Office and in other countries. Marca Registrada. Bantam Books, 1540
Broadway, New York, New York 10036.

PRINTED IN THE UNITED STATES OF AMERICA

OPM   10 9 8 7 6 5 4 3 2 1

For Dick

The light shines in the darkness, but the darkness has not understood it.

John 1:5

One

"The pink one? Or the red?" Nicole Brewster wondered aloud, holding up both sweaters. How could she choose when they created such entirely different effects? The pink was soft, fuzzy, and innocent; the red was tight and daring—and she was going to Hollywood, after all.

"The red one," she decided, putting the brand-new sweater into the suitcase she'd received for Christmas. "*And* the pink." She dropped that one in too, securing them both beneath fabric-covered elastic straps.

Most years Nicole wouldn't have considered a suitcase an exciting present. She'd have considered it a downright weird one, in fact, since she never managed to leave stifling little Clearwater Crossing, Missouri. But in light of Leah Rosenthal's recent invitation to accompany her, Jenna Conrad, and Melanie Andrews to the U.S. Girls modeling contest in California, the spiffy new suitcase had taken on extraordinary significance.

It's a sign. Forget coincidence. Forget her parents'

1

explanation that they were only thinking of building up her luggage for when she went off to college. Nicole knew better. She had asked God to send her a sign if she was on the wrong track with her dieting, and only two days later that sign had arrived: Leah had invited her to the contest and her parents had given her a suitcase.

Now I know I was right to lose so much weight. I'm probably going to be discovered by someone in L.A., she thought dreamily, wondering if she ought to pack a bikini. Everyone said it was sunny all year in southern California, but the contest *was* taking place in the middle of January. Nicole glanced through her bedroom window at the freezing gray Monday morning outside and shivered. How warm could it be?

A loud, split-second knock at her door snapped Nicole back to the present just as thirteen-year-old Heather walked in uninvited. "Hey, whatcha doing?"

Nicole winced, then decided not to make a big deal about it. With Heather, any type of knock was an improvement over her usual unannounced entrance. "If you would use your eyes instead of your mouth," Nicole said haughtily, "it would be obvious that I'm packing."

"For what? Not California! Give me a break, Nicole. That trip's still three weeks away."

"There's no point in waiting until the last minute."

"You're crazy! Your clothes will be all wrinkled if you leave them stuffed in there."

Nicole tossed her blond hair disdainfully but made a mental note to pack her mom's travel iron.

"Can't you find something better to do with your vacation?" Heather persisted.

Nicole ignored her sister with surprising ease. *Heather's just jealous*, she thought smugly, opening the dresser drawer where she kept her underwear and bikinis. *And rightly so*.

As eager as Nicole had once been to lounge around during the remaining week of winter break, now she could barely wait for school to start again the following Monday. Everyone was going to be so jealous! She couldn't wait to tell them all about her good luck.

Everyone but Courtney, that is. Her face fell a little at the thought. Even though Nicole had known about the trip since Christmas morning, she still hadn't mustered the courage to tell her best friend. Courtney was going to be furious that Jenna had been invited to the U.S. Girls finals instead of her, especially since Jenna had copped out on the preliminary contest—where Leah had won the Missouri title—while Courtney had sat through the whole long thing. Courtney had even gone so far as to suggest that Leah take three girlfriends as her guests, except that in Courtney's plan she was one of the three.

"Pam Springer's house got TP'ed last night," Heather announced, changing the subject as she dropped onto Nicole's unmade bed beside the open suitcase. "Wendy just called to tell me."

Burying each other's houses under toilet paper was the latest fad with the junior-high-school crowd. Nicole shook her head, grateful she was sixteen and more mature. "So what?"

Heather's gray eyes were excited. She smoothed back her unbrushed hair with one agitated hand. "Don't you get it? Only the *cool* people get toilet-papered. Being TP'ed, that's like . . . cool."

"More freezing than cool," said Nicole, gesturing toward the window. "Wouldn't summer be a better time to sneak around in the middle of the night?"

"It's not snowing."

That was true, and even the snow that had fallen on Christmas Eve had been reduced to dirty patches under trees and bushes. Even so . . .

"I would think you could find something better to do."

"Then you don't understand. It has to be hard—that's the whole point. If it were easy, it wouldn't mean anything."

Nicole shook her head again. It didn't mean anything anyway. The way Heather was talking, she seemed to think a person could read her future in toilet paper the way a fortune-teller read tea leaves.

"Whatever," she said, returning to her packing. She had barely reached for her turquoise tank top, though, when her mind went back to Courtney. *Maybe she won't be that mad. She wouldn't want to leave Jeff for three days anyway. Probably.*

4

"Pam's house is the third one this week," Heather said to Nicole's turned back. "First was Wynn Stanley, then Jeff Settner. Wow!"

" 'Wow' is right. Someone must be really bored."

"Huh? Oh, they weren't all done by the same person. I mean, I'd be really surprised. Whoever does it usually leaves a clue somewhere, so they can take credit later, when everyone's finished guessing. Tom Barrett did Wynn's house and nobody *ever* suspected *him*. It was so cool when he finally told her to look under her doormat for a little gold heart. They're going together now, you know. It's so romantic!"

Heather fell backward on the bed, overcome. Nicole rolled her eyes, unimpressed by the romantic capabilities of toilet paper.

Should I tell Courtney now, or should I wait until closer to the trip? she worried as Heather rambled on and on about the thrills and status-enhancing possibilities of pulping someone's house. Every cowardly fiber in Nicole's body urged her to postpone that awful moment as long as possible, but what if Courtney heard the news from someone else? Nicole shuddered involuntarily. *That would have to be worse.*

She almost wished she could just go to California and come back without Courtney ever knowing. But there was no way to hide such a big secret in such a small town. Sooner or later Courtney would find out . . . and then she'd be twice as mad.

I'll tell her this afternoon, Nicole vowed, refusing to remember that she'd already made the same resolution and chickened out the last two days in a row. *It'll be a relief to get it out of the way.*

"The thing is, though," Heather was still ranting, as if Nicole had been listening, "unless you're lucky enough to want to TP a person who lives on your street, someone has to drive you. And it's not exactly the kind of ride you can ask your parents for. . . . All the kids I know who've done it have really cool older brothers or sis—"

"Uh-huh," said Nicole, cutting Heather off impatiently and pointing toward the door. Now that she'd made up her mind about Courtney, she needed time to decide what to say.

A lot of time.

"You have to get out of here, Heathen. I'm busy."

"So, do you want to play another game of Maniac Marauders?" Ben Pipkin asked Mark Foster.

Mark shook his head and pushed an empty silver pizza tray farther away from him on their table. "No thanks. I'm too full to move."

Ben looked wistfully toward the bank of arcade games along the nearest wall of The Danger Zone. "Pushing a few buttons isn't exactly a workout."

"No. But how many times can you play the same game before it gets boring? Tomb of Terror is a lot more challenging."

Ben smiled, appreciative of the praise for the computer game his father had designed. On the other hand, he wouldn't have minded shooting up a few more bad guys either. His father never put guns in his games—too violent, he said. Ben could see his point, but it seemed like a fine line for a guy who didn't mind drownings, cave-ins, and big stone doors that could crush a man to death.

"So what do you want to do then?" he asked.

Mark looked around him and shrugged. "Relax. Enjoy the scenery."

"Scenery?" The Danger Zone was a dark, dirty barn of a room, with picnic-bench-style tables crammed randomly into the center and arcade games lining all four walls—not exactly scenic under the best of conditions. Add to that the sticky floor, half-eaten remnants of mediocre food, and unbussed greasy dishes, and a person had a view all right, just not a pretty one. If they weren't going to play the games, Ben didn't see any reason to hang around.

"Yeah. Scenery," Mark repeated, nodding toward a group of girls separated from them by several unoccupied tables.

It wasn't unusual for half of CCHS to pack into The Danger Zone after football games, but that Monday afternoon things were pretty tame. There were a lot of young guys running through rolls of quarters, but hardly anyone was sitting at the tables. Of the few people who were, most looked junior-high-aged

7

to Ben. The girls Mark had just indicated were freshmen, at best.

"You'd better ask their mommies before you make a move on that bunch," Ben said, feeling very clever and grown-up to have thought of such a cool remark. The buzz only lasted an instant.

"Geez, Ben. I'm only looking. When I kiss a girl, I like her to have all her permanent teeth."

When Mark kissed a girl? He said it as though it were something he did all the time. Until that moment, Ben had thought Mark was only a little cooler than he was. Now, in an instant, everything changed. If Mark made a habit of kissing girls, then he was way, way cooler than Ben. In fact, if Mark had kissed even *one* girl . . .

"Permanent teeth are good. That's all I was saying," Ben replied, hoping his voice wasn't really as high as it suddenly sounded.

"The oldest girl I ever kissed was nineteen," Mark reminisced. "Linda Faring. What a babe."

Nineteen! Ben wasn't even on speaking terms with any girls that age.

"How about you?" Mark asked.

"Huh? Oh! I've, uh, never kissed anyone quite that old," Ben stammered. That was no lie—it just wasn't the whole truth.

"You don't know what you're missing," Mark bragged, leaning back on the bench. "Older girls are the best."

8

"Yeah, well, I figure there'll be plenty of time for college girls in college. I might as well make the most of high-school girls for now—especially since our school has so many pretty ones."

"You're not kidding. Every one of our cheerleaders is hot. Have you ever noticed that? Not like other schools, where there's always at least one who can't compete."

Ben nodded miserably. He *had* noticed that. He especially noticed it every time he saw Angela Maldonado, the junior with the long, dark curls and the beauty mark next to her mouth.

"Melanie's the hottest, though," Mark said. "Man, you've got it made, hanging around in that group with her."

Ben smiled weakly, hoping to give the impression that he had planned the whole thing somehow. At this point he wasn't about to tell Mark that his only interest in Melanie was friendship.

"Is she seeing anyone?" Mark asked.

"I don't know." Ben glanced nervously at his watch. "Oh, wow. I have to leave if I'm going to catch the bus."

He managed to gather his gloves and hat with a certain amount of dignity, but on the bus ride home he felt like a stupid little boy. He didn't want to blow his new friendship with Mark, but what would Mark think when he found out Ben had never kissed a girl?

Actually, Ben had kind of assumed Mark knew

that. The truth was, he'd assumed Mark was in the same boat. How unfair that Mark—a sophomore not much cooler or more popular than Ben was—had not only kissed a girl, he'd kissed a woman!

Ben hung his head and braced it against the back of the empty bus seat in front of him. His mom had offered to drive him to The Danger Zone and pick him up later, but he had declined for fear of looking immature.

Ha! he told himself now. *Being driven around by your mother is barely the tip of the iceberg.*

The wind cut through Melanie's corduroy coat, making her wish she had worn her parka. The sun had peeked out earlier, bringing the temperature into the fifties, but now the clouds choked it out again, like cold gray fingers snuffing a candle. Reluctantly Melanie turned away from the creek that wound through the woods at the back of her property and began trudging through the fields toward her house.

She had started her walk with the intention of trying to resolve some of the things on her mind, but she hadn't accomplished her goal. Lately it seemed as though she could barely concentrate on one problem before her distracted mind skipped over to something else. Half the time she didn't even realize she'd switched subjects. There were just so many things to sort out. . . .

Like her crazy Christmas Eve trip to Iowa to see

her mother's grave. That had happened only a few days before, but already it seemed half lost in the past. Melanie shook her head. Not only hadn't the trip put her mind at ease, the memory was kind of embarrassing now. Everything would have been okay if she could have figured out a way to go on her own and keep the experience to herself. But Jesse Jones had had to drive her and, thanks to a careless slip on her part, her father had found out.

Melanie hated having people know her business. It made her feel exposed, betrayed in a way she couldn't explain. When she controlled what people knew about her, she controlled the way they saw her. But as soon as anyone had the real facts . . .

I never should have left Clearwater Crossing, she thought with a sigh, kicking a lump of half-frozen dirt at the side of the path. It rolled into the dead brown grass and disappeared.

Except that maybe I do feel kind of better.

She hadn't really resolved anything, but she had made an effort. If there *was* any sort of life after death, she hoped her mother knew she had tried.

And it was hard to be sure, but maybe things would be a little better with her dad now too. He had promised to try to stop drinking, and even though she could tell he already regretted those words, he had made a few telephone calls that morning to fancy rehab places. Melanie wasn't convinced that finding exactly the right location to stop drinking wasn't just another form of stalling, but at least he was doing *something*.

In the meantime, there was the trip to California with Leah, Nicole, and Jenna to look forward to. Her father had given her his permission to go immediately, just as Melanie had known he would. She'd been able to call Leah back and confirm on Christmas morning, less than an hour after she'd been invited. Melanie wondered what Hollywood would be like. She hoped it would be fun, but she didn't much care. She'd have signed up for anything that got her away from her life for a while.

Skirting the wall that divided the swimming pool and poolhouse from the rest of the property, she walked the short remaining distance to her front door. As she reached the doorstep, her eyes glanced involuntarily toward the spot where she'd found Jesse's unexpected present.

"Jesse," she groaned to herself. There was another can of worms. On Christmas she had decided to give him a chance, but she'd been going back and forth on that idea ever since. She had really expected him to call by now, or even drop by. It hadn't seemed likely he would give her such an expensive gift without wanting anything in return. But his failure to follow up was working oddly in his favor. The longer he stayed away, the more possible it seemed to have him around.

Melanie yanked the front door open and shrugged

off her coat, enjoying the feeling of warm air on her cold nose. The Andrews place cost a fortune to heat, with its lofty ceilings and huge expanses of glass, but the furnace ran continuously in the winter anyway. Melanie's mother hadn't liked to be cold, and now nobody did.

Putting her coat in the entryway closet, Melanie climbed the curving marble staircase to her second-floor bedroom.

On the nightstand next to her bed, the porcelain angel Jesse had given her for Christmas held a place beside a new cordless phone from her father. Picking up the figurine, she examined its details: the delicate face and hands, the long golden hair, the translucent wing tips.

"What was he thinking?" she wondered aloud. She had to admit she was dying to know.

Melanie glanced at the phone again, then slowly put the angel down. She supposed she could give in and call him, since that seemed to be his game. The new white plastic was smooth in her hand as she lifted the handset from its base. She had programmed all of Eight Prime's numbers into the Speed Dial function on Christmas afternoon. If she wanted Jesse, all she had to do was press three buttons, and there was very little doubt he'd come running.

She started to put the phone down, then raised it again.

Would she be absolutely crazy to call him?

Two

"Whoa! Whoa, Whizzer!" Jenna shouted, barely maintaining a two-handed grip on the leash through her clumsy padded gloves. "Stop pulling! You'll knock me down."

Caitlin laughed at her side as they walked through the icy field behind Dr. Campbell's office. "I told you he was a wild boy. Want to switch?"

Jenna glanced from the out-of-control greyhound straining at the end of her leash to the small, pink-sweatered poodle trotting docilely on Caitlin's. She hadn't wanted to be seen with any dog who would wear such a goofy crocheted number, but old Fifi was looking better every minute. "All right."

Caitlin made the switch, and Jenna was relieved to feel her shoulders settle back into their sockets.

Caitlin was doing well with her dog-walking business—so well that she was starting to squeeze walks into her lunch break from the veterinarian's office in addition to her regular circuit after work and on weekends. Jenna had offered to help that Tuesday afternoon simply for the company and the exercise—except that she hadn't anticipated quite so *much* exercise.

"Granola bar?" Caitlin offered, miraculously managing to hold Whizzer's leash with one hand while reaching into her parka pocket.

Jenna shook her head. "Is that your whole lunch? Granola bars?"

"For now. I'll get back to Dr. Campbell's a few minutes early and eat my yogurt."

"So where do you usually take these guys?" Jenna asked, nodding toward the dogs.

"Around. It doesn't much matter as long as they get to stretch their legs." The dogs lived a couple of blocks from Dr. Campbell's office, making them perfect candidates for a lunchtime outing. "I was thinking we could probably get as far as Peter's and back in plenty of time."

"Peter's?" Jenna repeated, perking up.

"If you want to. You could tell him those pictures Dad took of the two of you are supposed to be ready today."

"Good idea." Peter had been so busy doing things with his visiting older brother, David, that for the last three days Jenna's contact with him had been reduced to telephone calls. She hadn't seen him since Christmas morning, when he'd come to her house to pose for pictures with her.

At least he had still been over when Leah had called with her big news—Jenna was invited to the

U.S. Girls contest! It would have been too cruel if she hadn't been able to share her excitement with Peter in person, even though the Conrads' permission was still contingent upon Mrs. Conrad's checking out the arrangements. Days had passed since then, though, and Jenna was happy for any excuse to see Peter. Altering direction, she quickened her steps eagerly.

From the sidewalk in front of the Altmanns' house, the girls heard voices in the garage. They took the dogs around to the side door and knocked.

David Altmann opened the door almost immediately, waving them into the garage. "Hey, come on in! I didn't know you girls had dogs now."

Shy Caitlin blushed and looked at the floor, leaving Jenna to answer for both of them. "Caitlin does have a dog now, but it's at home. These dogs are part of her dog-walking business."

David raised an eyebrow that was the exact same shape as Peter's. "You have your own business? Way to go!"

"It's really small," Caitlin mumbled modestly.

Jenna rolled her eyes and walked over to Peter. He was standing beside the Altmanns' old Tercel, wiping his greasy hands on a rag. The car's hood was propped up and tools were strewn about everywhere. Apparently he and David had been working on the engine.

"We're giving it a tuneup," Peter explained, reading the question in her eyes. "New spark plugs, antifreeze, that kind of thing."

16

"Is it still running?"

"Of course. I'm picking you up for the meeting, right?"

"Right," Jenna agreed happily, looking forward to finally having some time with him. Leah was holding her first Eight Prime meeting that night, at her condominium. "But do you think you could come over a little early? My dad's supposed to get those pictures of us back today."

"The Christmas ones? Oh, good."

David and Caitlin moved over beside them.

"So where's Mary Beth?" David asked. "Did she go back to school already?"

Jenna shook her head. "She's out with friends today."

And every day, she couldn't help adding to herself. The oldest Conrad girl was supposed to be visiting her family during her winter break from college, but it seemed as if she was visiting everyone else in town instead.

"When are you going back?" Caitlin asked.

David leaned against the car. "Sunday morning, after church."

"That's when Mary Beth's leaving too, so you'll probably run into her again before you go," Jenna said, pulling the curious poodle away from a spot of oil on the concrete floor.

David nodded, then reached under the hood to adjust something. Jenna watched for a moment, temporarily distracted by how much he looked like Peter—an older, blonder, Peter, of course, with far more muscular arms. . . . As if David sensed her attention, he glanced up suddenly, giving her a questioning look.

"Well! I guess we'd better be heading back. Uh, right, Caitlin?" Jenna blurted, mortified. She hadn't really been checking David out. But what if he thought she had?

"Yes. My lunch break's almost over," Caitlin murmured.

"I'm glad you came by," Peter told Jenna, smiling.

"Yeah," David said. "I hope I'll see all of you girls again before I leave."

Jenna was still so flustered that her face felt hot enough to fry pancakes on. "I'm sure you will," she said quickly. "In fact, I have an idea—why don't you both come to dinner at our house tomorrow?" She'd have said anything she thought would get her out of that garage one second sooner.

David and Peter glanced at each other, then nodded in unison. "Okay."

"Great. Well, see you tomorrow then. Except for you, Peter. I'll see you tonight."

Somehow she got her poodle maneuvered out the side door and down to the sidewalk again, where the chilly air cooled her cheeks and brought her back to her senses.

Caitlin joined her with the greyhound. "You

probably should have asked Mom before you invited company to dinner," she said softly.

"Probably," Jenna agreed. She could hardly tell her sister she had totally panicked—or why. Especially since the whole thing seemed so silly now. She *definitely* hadn't been checking David out; it was just kind of interesting to see how Peter might look in a few more years.

"Well, maybe she won't mind. But if you want to, you can say we both invited them."

"You mean it?" Jenna asked gratefully. Their mom would be a lot less likely to get mad at Caitlin for having uninvited guests, since Caitlin never had guests at all. "Thanks, Cat. You're the best."

Caitlin shrugged, embarrassed. "What are sisters for?"

"So, does everyone agree?" Leah asked tensely, wondering how she'd ended up in the position of mediator. Just because they were holding the Eight Prime meeting in her living room didn't mean she wanted to be in charge. "Are we going with Melanie's design?"

She looked around for dissenters, but everyone was nodding. "Okay, then. I guess that's it." Leah handed the drawings to Peter, Melanie's on top of the stack.

The vote had been to decide how to paint Kurt Englbehrt's name on the bus they had bought for an

19

underprivileged kids' group in his memory. Everyone had drawn up their ideas for honoring their classmate and brought them that night, but—demonstrating the principle that simpler is better—Melanie's had won. Her design consisted of navy blue block lettering on both sides of the sky blue bus:

REMEMBERING KURT ENGLBEHRT

"I still think it would look prettier if we did the same thing in pink," Nicole grumbled.

"Trust me," Jesse said, "Kurt would prefer blue. The guy was a football player, not a ballerina."

"Well, we all just voted for blue anyway. Right?" Leah said, glancing desperately at Peter.

"Right," he said quickly, taking over at last. "I'll see if Chris can drive the bus to Signs of the Times tomorrow. That's the shop that gave me the quotes."

"Are we going to have enough money?" Ben asked.

Peter nodded. "Melanie's design looks easy, so it ought to be pretty cheap. We should be okay, but we won't have a lot left over."

"If there's any extra, I think we should spend it on sports equipment for the Junior Explorers," said Jesse. "That sled I bought to replace the one Jason lost was a killer deal, and there's all kinds of other stuff on sale now too."

"Good idea!" said Ben. "Let's spend all our money.

We can do a fund-raiser to make some more when the girls get back from California."

Leah stared at him, amazed he already knew about that. But, judging by the way everyone else was taking the information in stride, the rest of the guys knew too. *Well, of course they do,* she thought, irrationally irritated by the mention of the U.S. Girls contest. *I told Miguel, Jenna told Peter, and anyone could have told Jesse and Ben.*

"What kind of fund-raiser should we do?" Jenna asked, her pink pen poised.

"Let's think about it later," Nicole said. "That's so far away."

"Hey, is everyone going to the New Year's Eve party at Jon Young's house?" Jesse asked. Jon was dating Brooke Henderson, senior class president and homecoming queen, so everyone knew who he was. "It sounds like half the school's going to be there."

"What party?" Ben asked eagerly.

Jesse made a face, as if he should have known better.

"Jon is having an open party," Melanie explained. "If you want to go, all you have to do is show up."

"Really? Are you guys all going?"

"We are," Miguel answered, sliding his arm around Leah. A playful squeeze of her ribs told her he was ready to end the meeting.

She stood up abruptly, happy to oblige. She'd volunteered her condo that night more out of a sense of duty than any real desire to wedge eight people into the Rosenthals' small living room. If her parents hadn't elected to stay in their bedroom, things would have been really crowded.

"So, I guess that's it, then," Leah said, hoping people would take the hint. They did. A moment later everyone was up and putting on coats. "I'll walk you downstairs," she whispered to Miguel, holding on to his hand to keep him from leaving with the others. They waited a few minutes, until they were sure of having the lobby to themselves, then took the elevator down to the first floor.

"What do you want to do tomorrow?" he asked, putting his arms around her. "Should we see a movie? All the matinees are half price."

Leah shook her head. "I can't. I didn't get a single thing done today."

"Like what?" he asked, laughing. "It's vacation."

"You know I have to finish filling out my college applications. I have two left, and they're both due in a couple of days."

A trace of annoyance flickered across Miguel's handsome face. "Why do they need those stupid things so early? It's ridiculous."

"Are you working on yours?" she asked hopefully.

"My one big application? I think I can still crank it out in time. Clearwater University gives you until March, as you ought to know, with both of your parents teaching there."

"Yes, but . . ." *But all the good schools have deadlines around the first of the year.* She'd had to apply to Stanford—her top choice—before mid-December. "If you don't do something by tomorrow, CU will be your only option. You have to apply to a few different places to give yourself something to choose from."

"I do have something to choose from." The look in his brown eyes hinted at his old stubbornness. "I can still go to City College for the first two years to do my general ed. I'll probably do that anyway. Why should I pay good money for classes that are practically free at City?"

"Why?" So many answers popped into her head at once that she didn't know which one to pick. "I guess . . . Well . . . It's not just about the classes, Miguel. College is an *experience*, and—"

"Experiences cost money, Leah." His expression warned her not to bring up need-based scholarships and financial aid again. "Besides, it's amazing enough that I'm going to college at all. I don't need to be picky."

But you can *be picky. You* should *be picky!* Leah had to bite back the words she wanted to shout. "I can't afford half the schools I want either, Miguel," she said instead. "If I don't win the U.S. Girls scholarship, I can probably kiss my top choices good-bye. But it's just stupid not to apply."

His heavy eyebrows drew together.

"I'm sorry, but it is," she rushed on determinedly.

"No one can say what's going to happen between now and fall. And I know you don't want to hear it, but financial aid is a fact of life. My family's not rich, Miguel. If I get offered any, I'll take it in a heartbeat and be grateful."

"Yeah, well, that's you," he grumbled.

Their eyes locked. The argument was a standoff. And Leah felt her heart sink.

Maybe Miguel's college plan wasn't so bad. Maybe it even made sense. For Miguel. But there was no way that after a lifetime of dreaming of the best, Leah could settle for Clearwater University—especially not with both of her parents working there. College was supposed to be about getting out, growing up, cutting the apron strings . . . not living at home and riding to classes with Mommy and Daddy.

But if she left Clearwater Crossing, she'd be leaving Miguel too.

Even the thought was painful.

No, she decided stubbornly, snuggling into his arms. *He still has two days to fill out applications. I'll just have to convince him to go to a good school.*

Three

"When I was your age, I could have reached that cobweb without a ladder," Charlie Johnson told Jesse from the crushed-down seat of his brown recliner.

Any other day the comment might have annoyed him, but that Wednesday Jesse wasn't just on top of Charlie's rickety old stepladder, he was on top of the world. The fact that it had been too cold and wet outside to do any yard work, the fact that he was having to work off the remainder of his community service sentence indoors with Charlie observing his every move, even the fact that all the old guy did was talk, talk, talk . . . none of those things could get him down.

He was closer to having Melanie than he'd ever thought he'd get.

"Sure, Charlie, you were eight feet tall."

"I could jump. For your information, I could jump four feet straight up from a standstill."

Jesse turned around on the ladder and surveyed the senior citizen. The guy couldn't even get from the living room to the kitchen without a walker, and the way he hunched over its aluminum frame put the top of his head somewhere below Jesse's shoulder. "Yeah. Right, Charlie."

Once again Jesse wished there were something he could do to keep busy outside. If conditions had been drier he could have cut weeds, but an afternoon thaw had turned the ground to mush. If there had been any snow, he could have shoveled the walk, but no snow had fallen since Christmas Eve. He looked longingly toward the window and all he saw was the same unrelieved grayness that had gripped the town for days. Sighing, he climbed down from the ladder, the remains of the spiderweb clinging to a crumpled paper towel.

"You think you're such an athlete, don't you?" Charlie demanded with uncharacteristic bitterness. "Well, let me tell you something: Everything you can do, I could do better." His piercing blue eyes held Jesse's from across the room, and a stray lock of white hair fell onto his shriveled forehead as he strained forward to make his point.

The sight gave Jesse the creeps. "Sure, Charlie. Whatever. Listen, I'm going to put this ladder back." Quickly folding up the stepladder, he tucked it under one arm and headed for the kitchen.

There's got to be something I can do in here, he thought as he shoved the stepladder into its place beside the refrigerator.

He glanced at his watch, then reluctantly in the direction of the living room. He had already been there six hours. If he could just kill an hour more, he could knock out the rest of his forty-hour commitment by shoveling Charlie's walks after the next good snow. Not that Charlie was likely to use them in his condition, but hey—a deal was a deal. As long as Jesse did *something* at Charlie's for forty hours, he would finally be square with Coach Davis for the drinking incident that had gotten him temporarily kicked off the school football team.

With a sigh, Jesse pulled the stepladder back out, got a wet sponge, and climbed up to remove a century's dust from the top of the refrigerator. Anything was better than going back out to the living room and listening to Charlie.

"What are you doing in there?" Charlie called irritably.

"Cleaning your refrigerator," Jesse called back, getting a new idea: After he did the outside, he could do the inside too.

"It doesn't need it."

"Not much, it doesn't." Jesse flipped on the kitchen radio to discourage further conversation and focused his thoughts on Melanie.

She'd been checking him out at the Eight Prime meeting the night before. He'd seen her doing it. She'd been playing it cool, of course, but not as cool as he had. All during the meeting, from the opening chitchat to the final vote on the bus design, she'd been sneaking looks his way. And eventually curiosity had gotten the better of her.

I knew it would work! he thought triumphantly. *I was a genius to remember that old look-alike angel of mine.*

Waiting in the car while Melanie visited her mother's grave, he had seen her bury something in the snow. Later, when she'd fled into the cemetery chapel, he hadn't been able to resist. Hurrying to the headstone, he had scraped back the snow just enough to see the delicate angel ornament Melanie had placed there before he carefully reburied it. He'd found the sight strangely sad. But as the day had worn on, the sadness had been replaced by a creeping feeling of déjà vu. He'd seen that angel before. . . .

And then he'd remembered. When he was a boy, his mother had put one just like it on top of his dresser. He'd been very little then—too little to protest that angels were for girls—and besides, there had been something oddly comforting about the way his night-light glowed through the angel's wide wings. As soon as he'd been old enough, though, the delicate porcelain figure had been banished to a box at the back of his closet. Over the years that followed, so many baseballs and books and trophies took turns in the angel's place that he gradually forgot he'd ever owned it. He wasn't even sure its box had made the trip from California to Missouri. But eventually he had found it on a storage shelf in the garage and hurriedly ripped off the packing tape. The figurine inside was even more like Melanie's angel than he'd remembered, and absolutely perfect in every detail—not a single scratch or chip marred its glossy surface anywhere. And, for a moment, the old memento had reminded him so strongly of his mother that he'd almost changed his mind about giving it to Melanie. In the end, of course, he'd come to his senses—and was he ever glad he had! The gift had softened Melanie up more than anything else he'd ever done.

The angel had only been phase one of his plan, though. The next step—the harder step—had been to ignore her the last few days to give her time to think. He'd been pretty sure she wouldn't call him, and he'd been right, but four or five times a day he'd had to stop himself from reaching for his own phone or—worse—his car keys. All the effort had been worth it, though. She was totally interested now. He had read it in her eyes when she'd thanked him for the figurine after the Eight Prime meeting.

"No problem. Glad you like it," he'd said, his phrases made breezy by days of practice. "So, are you going to Jon's party?"

She'd shrugged and twisted one of the rings on her fingers. "I guess. All the cheerleaders are going." Then, after a pause: "Are you?"

He smiled now at the memory as he wrung out the

filthy sponge in Charlie's sink. Was he going? Was she kidding? That party was phase three of his plan.

"Jesse, you come on out here," Charlie called impatiently. "I want to show you something."

Not another cobweb, Jesse groaned to himself.

In my day, I didn't need a ladder, he mocked Charlie silently as he shuffled out to the living room. *Heck, if I just gave those spiders the eye, they sucked their webs back into their rumps and ran.*

"Yeah? What is it?" Jesse asked resignedly.

"Here." Charlie was still sitting in his worn chair, but somehow he had gotten his veined hands on a framed photograph Jesse had never seen before. The old man thrust the picture insistently forward, waiting for Jesse to take it.

Jesse couldn't suppress a gasp.

The photograph showed a young, broad-shouldered man posing in the long-ago uniform of an NFL team. The black-and-white print had faded, but the piercing eyes that challenged the camera were unmistakable. Hand-lettered across the bottom in fancy calligraphy were the words *Charlie Johnson, #88, Chicago Bears*.

"I made it pretty far," Charlie said. "Far enough not to take any crap off a high-school kid. Your attitude's going to be your downfall, Jesse."

"My attitude!" Jesse protested, amazed that someone as difficult as Charlie would dare to criticize him. "What's wrong with my attitude?"

"Change it, or you'll find out. I know, because mine was exactly the same." Charlie glanced away a moment, then fixed his gaze back on Jesse.

"You'd better believe I thought I was something once. No one could tell me anything. And as long as I kept playing like I was on fire, that was all I cared about. But the month after they took that picture, I ripped a knee. The next season, I tore the other one—blew it completely apart. And that was the end of football. Just like that."

"What did you do?"

"The problem was, I didn't know how to do anything else. Except drink. And I got a whole lot better at that. What else was there? That's what I told myself, anyway. When I finally figured out what an idiot I'd been, I'd already wasted half my life. And my health, well . . ."

Charlie shook his head. "What I know now is I could have done anything. There were a thousand possibilities, if I'd only been smart enough to see them. Do you understand what I'm trying to tell you?"

"Yes," Jesse squeezed out past the awed lump in his throat.

"Keep the photo," Charlie said. "You might need it sometime."

There was no longer any doubt in Jesse's mind that Coach Davis had set him up. There was no school rule about doing community service, and the coach hadn't just grabbed Charlie's name out of a hat somewhere. He had hooked Jesse up with Charlie Johnson one hundred percent on purpose.

The odd thing was, Jesse didn't mind anymore. "You and Coach Davis . . . you know each other, don't you?"

Charlie tried to smile. "Used to. He's my son."

"Benny, why are you lollygagging around back there?" his mother asked irritably. Turning her head, she peered back over her shoulder, still pushing her shopping cart forward through the local Value-Mart. "Walk up here where I can see you."

Ben stifled a groan. Wasn't it bad enough that she'd been dragging him on her errands all afternoon? Did he have to trot at her side like a total mama's boy?

You are a mama's boy, he told himself miserably, taking a few steps to catch up. *And no one can miss your mama.*

Mrs. Pipkin had been overweight before Ben was born, but since then she'd been putting on pounds so steadily and so reliably that a person looking through the family photo albums could practically guess the date by the size of her upper arms. Every year her doctor told her to lose weight, and every year she gained. Balanced above her open winter coat, her turban-wrapped head seemed too small for her body, like a pea atop a grapefruit. Ben loved his mother, but as he took his place at her side that afternoon, he couldn't help hoping that no one from school would see them.

"All the Christmas decorations are going to be dirt cheap now," Mrs. Pipkin said, pushing her cart around an enormous display of potato chips. "I want to see what I can put away for next year."

The Christmas aisle looked as though a meteor had struck it. Red and green decorations were strewn in every direction, including all over the floor. Ben's mother weaved her cart slowly through the wreckage, keeping a lookout for bargains. She was so intent on the price of gift wrap that she didn't even see the twenty-something couple at the other end of the aisle, kissing under the plastic mistletoe.

But Ben did. Everywhere he'd gone for the last two days, ever since his discussion with Mark, he'd noticed people kissing. In the mall, on the bus, outside the video store at night . . . *For Pete's sake, even in Value-Mart*, he thought, glaring at the happy couple. They seemed to feel the heat of his stare, because they finally looked up, laughed, and moved on.

His mother picked up a mechanical Santa and began examining it.

It's just because of the holidays, he tried to reassure himself. *Goodwill toward men and all that.*

So how come no one ever felt that sort of goodwill toward *him*? The whole never-kissed-a-girl thing was starting to drive him crazy.

Especially since Mark had! There was something

completely unfair about that. Ben took it for granted that everyone in Eight Prime had kissed someone . . . but why Mark and not him? They were practically the same—except that Mark was kissing nineteen-year-olds.

Ben had been on a date once, in junior high school. Mary Alwin had asked him to the movies. But he hadn't kissed her. He hadn't even *tried* to kiss her. At the time he'd been in a total sweat just thinking of holding her hand. Which, of course, he also hadn't managed.

But now he was almost sixteen, and it was embarrassing to be so inexperienced when all around him everyone else was growing up. The way he was headed, he was going to be the last unkissed person in Clearwater Crossing.

Probably in the whole world.

"I could set the table if you want," Caitlin offered as Jenna hurried toward the oven with a cookie sheet full of cold rolls.

"Yes. No, wait! Isn't it Sarah's turn?" Jenna tried to set the oven timer while simultaneously reading the chore schedule posted on the refrigerator. Peter and David would be arriving for dinner any minute, and Jenna needed Caitlin's help too badly to let her do Sarah's chores.

"I just thought—"

"No. Make Sarah do it. Sarah!" Jenna bellowed,

turning her head in the general direction of Sarah's downstairs bedroom. "It's time to set the table!"

No reply.

"Do you think she heard me?" Jenna asked Caitlin.

"She heard you," Mary Beth said, wandering in from the living room. Despite the fact that company was coming, she was wearing faded overalls and a stretched-out sweater, and her coppery curls spilled in all directions from a scrunchie on top of her head. "They probably heard you next door."

"Well, is she going to do it?"

"Yeah, yeah, in a minute. Stop being such a little dictator."

Mary Beth looked over the food assembled on the kitchen counter, selected a carrot stick, and dragged it right through the middle of the dip Caitlin had just arranged into a perfect swirl of white.

"Mary Beth!" Jenna squealed. "That's for the guests!"

"Ooh, sor-ry!" Mary Beth said sarcastically, sounding exactly like Maggie. "I thought I *was* a guest."

That's pretty obvious. Jenna had to bite her lip to keep from saying so out loud. Ever since her oldest sister had come home from school, all she had done was run off with her friends or lounge around the house expecting to be waited on. Jenna had tried to be patient, but Mary Beth was really starting to rub her the wrong way.

Tonight, for example. She could have helped me and

Caitlin. It's not like she's doing *anything—except mess-ing up the dip.*

When Jenna had told her mother about impul-sively inviting Peter and David to dinner, Mrs. Conrad had taken the news surprisingly well. Too well.

"Oh, good," she'd said excitedly. "I was looking for a reason not to cook tomorrow."

"Huh?" Jenna had turned to Caitlin, but Caitlin had shrugged, equally confused.

"Since you've invited guests, of course you'll be cooking for them. And it's as easy to make dinner for ten as for four. Let me know what we're having."

"Uh, okay," Jenna had said, reeling. "Sure."

"I'll help you," Caitlin had whispered immediately.

But Mary Beth had only laughed. "Way to go, Jenna," she'd teased. "I hope Peter likes Hamburger Helper."

"I hope you do," Jenna had retorted.

But it hadn't come to that. With Caitlin's help, Jenna had cooked up a delicious-looking roast beef, along with baked potatoes, broccoli, and an apple pie for dessert. *Well, okay, so I bought the pie,* she thought. *The point is that Mary Beth didn't do a single thing.*

"Don't you need to be somewhere else?" she asked her sister now. "No offense, Mary Beth, but you know what they say: Either lead, follow, or get out of the way."

Mary Beth smiled smugly. "Then I'll gladly get out of the way. This *is* my vacation, you know."

Jenna glared at her sister's retreating back. "If she says that one more time . . . ," she grumbled dangerously to Caitlin. "She keeps reminding us that it's her vacation like the rest of us only have time off to make her comfortable. I'm on vacation too, you know."

"She doesn't mean it like that," Caitlin said quickly. "That's just Mary Beth."

Caitlin's defense hurt almost more than Mary Beth's behavior. Mary Beth had been Caitlin's favorite once, but Jenna had thought she'd moved into that place. Now Caitlin was taking Mary Beth's side against her.

Jenna took a deep breath, determined not to be petty. "I really appreciate your helping me out with dinner tonight," she said. "I mean it. I couldn't have done it without you."

"It was nothing," Caitlin murmured, embarrassed. "It was half my fault you got stuck cooking, anyway."

"What? No way! I'm the one who opened my big mouth without asking Mom first."

Caitlin turned pink, then lifted her nose and sniffed the air. "Are those rolls burning?"

"Oh, wow!" Grabbing a hot pad, Jenna launched herself across the kitchen just as the doorbell rang.

"I'll get it!" Mary Beth trilled from the living room.

Jenna yanked the oven door open. The rolls were fine.

"Oh, sure. We do all the work and she grabs all the glory," she complained, shoveling the rolls into a basket with a spatula. "She could have asked if one of *us* wanted to answer the door."

"I can finish up in here," Caitlin offered. "Go say hi to Peter."

Jenna pushed the last roll off the sheet. "Really?"

Just then Peter's laugh rang out in the entryway, echoed by David's deeper, slightly more restrained one. Jenna hurried to wash her hands. She knew she ought to stay and do the last few things herself, but she'd hardly seen Peter at all lately. And if Caitlin didn't mind . . .

"Thanks, Cat," she said, flashing her sister a smile before she threw down the dish towel and ran toward the living room. "You really are the best."

"Can I have more cake?" Heather asked hopefully, holding out her plate.

"No, you *may* not," Mrs. Brewster replied sternly. "Really, Heather, if you keep eating this way, you're going to be big as a house."

Nicole smirked and savored her superiority. She hadn't accepted even a sliver of cake, and more of her dinner had been pushed around her plate than actually consumed. She'd been cutting herself too much slack lately, foolishly taking advice from all the wrong people, but now that she was sure she was destined to be a model, she was back on her diet with a vengeance.

"Let Heather have my piece," she offered grandly. "I couldn't eat another bite."

Instead of acting appreciative, Heather rolled her eyes. "More like another nibble. Never mind. I couldn't take food from the starving."

Mrs. Brewster looked from one to the other and then pointedly changed the subject. "Some teenage vandal covered the Smiths' house with toilet paper last night," she said, directing her remark to her husband. "When I went out to the market this morning, you could barely see it under all that mess."

Nicole glanced questioningly at Heather, but her sister just smiled and shook her head slightly to show she didn't know who had done it.

"Oh, well," Mr. Brewster replied. "At least it kept those Smith boys busy in their own yard for a while, cleaning up. I don't know what it is, but there's something about those kids I just don't like."

"Then you're the only one, Dad," Heather butted in. "They're really popular at school."

Mrs. Brewster stared Heather down until she squirmed. "Is this something your friends are doing? Because it's a filthy waste of time. If anyone ever messes up *this* house—"

"Pay attention, Mom," Nicole interrupted. "You have to be *popular* to get TP'ed. Heather couldn't be safer. Look, can I be excused? I have to go call Courtney."

"You can watch your tone," Mrs. Brewster said icily. "And then you can clear the table."

By the time Nicole finally got up to her bedroom, all the joy of zinging Heather had worn off. And it wasn't because she'd been made to clear the table—she'd have had to do that anyway. She was worrying about what she'd say to Courtney.

"You should've told her yesterday," she muttered to herself, toying with the antenna on the phone.

She and Courtney had spent almost the entire day at the mall, and there had been a million opportunities. All Nicole would have had to do was point at something—*anything*—and say, "Oh, how cute. That would be perfect for my trip to California." She wouldn't have had to volunteer any more than that; Courtney would have pulled the rest of the story out of her in nothing flat.

"Oh, well. Should've, could've, would've," Nicole muttered, dialing the telephone. "I'll just have to tell her now."

Courtney picked up on the first ring. "Jeff?" she said eagerly.

"Sorry to disappoint you. Do you want me to call back later?"

"What for?"

"Well, I mean if you were waiting for Jeff or something . . ."

"Oh. No, that's all right. I just got off the phone with him."

40

"Okay," Nicole said slowly, completely confused. Then she shrugged, too preoccupied with the reason she'd called to care about anything else. *Start with a warm-up question*, she thought.

"Are you guys still picking me up for the party tomorrow?"

"Huh? Sure. Nicole, do you think I'm sarcastic?"

"Sarcastic? You?" Nicole exclaimed, laughing at her own joke. "Of course. Why do you ask?"

"I don't know. Just something Jeff said."

"Did you two have a fight?"

"No," Courtney said irritably. "Why did you call me, anyway?"

"Uh, no reason," Nicole lied quickly. Her topic had to be eased into gradually, not blurted out on the spur of the moment. Especially not when the person being blurted to was obviously in such a bad mood. Maybe now wasn't the right time after all.

I have to tell her before the party, though. If I don't, she'll find out there for sure.

Still, the New Year's Eve party didn't start until eight the next night.

And that leaves me a whole day.

Four

"What about this one?" Leah asked, handing Miguel another fancy college brochure. "This is a really good school, and it's not as expensive as some of the others."

Miguel barely glanced at the glossy, ivy-covered buildings on the cover before he tossed the pamphlet onto the coffee table. "Next. Unless you have something without ivy, I don't think I'm interested. Where are the real schools for regular people like me?"

Leah leaned forward on the del Rioses' small sofa and began digging through the messy stacks of brochures, catalogs, and extra applications she'd brought with her. Mrs. del Rios was working that New Year's Eve day, filling in as holiday help at the department store where she'd held a full-time job before she got ill, and Rosa was off with friends. Leah and Miguel had his house to themselves—the first time that had ever happened. Conditions for tempting Miguel with her college plan couldn't have been more perfect.

Except that he wasn't interested. Leah tried not to betray her growing desperation as she sifted through the materials in front of her, looking for anything he hadn't already seen. "They're *all* real schools," she said, pretending not to know what he meant. "They're the best schools in the country."

Miguel glanced at his watch. "It feels weird to have my mom off at work for so long. Between her job at church and all the hours she's picked up at the store this week, she's practically full-time again."

"But that's great." Leah hesitated. "Isn't it?"

"Are you kidding? It's fantastic! With the money she's making now and what I'm about to bring in, we'll be out of this dump by summer."

"This house is not a dump."

"You know what I mean."

She nodded. He meant he hated living in public housing, taking assistance from the government. But why had he brought that up now? Was he only making conversation, or was that his way of telling her to drop the college discussion?

"I can't believe you're taking a job *now*," she said, temporarily distracted. "I thought your mother didn't want you to work while you were still in school."

Miguel smiled. "Well, I'm going to be in school a lot longer now, aren't I? Besides, this was too good to pass up. Mr. Ambrosi was a friend of my dad's, so I know he'll treat me right. And painting can be good money. Actually, I'm looking forward to it."

I'm glad somebody is, Leah thought sourly. She didn't want to be selfish, but it already felt as if the clock

43

were running out on them. And with Miguel starting work the following week, he was going to have a lot less free time in the afternoons too.

"How about this?" she asked, snatching blindly at a brochure near the bottom of the stack.

Miguel surveyed it with bored eyes. "Seen it. How about *this*?"

Spinning around on the sofa, he pounced, knocking her backward into the cushions and simultaneously reaching under her sweater to tickle her ribs. She struggled a moment, then pushed his hands away. "Seen it," she said petulantly.

Miguel raised one eyebrow. "Well, then. I guess I don't have anything left to show you. Except maybe this."

Leaning over her again, he stopped with their faces an inch apart. His eyes bored into hers. And then he kissed her. Slowly, deliberately, their eyes still connected. Leah felt her heart start to melt, but not the way it usually did. This time she felt only sadness. A great aching sadness that swelled inside her, threatening to fill the emptiness his absence would bring. She put her arms around him, buried her hands in his dark hair, and closed her eyes tight.

"Leah," she heard him whisper huskily. She pressed up against him, tightening her grip. "Leah . . ."

"Ow!"

Her eyes flew open to see him rubbing his scalp

with one hand. "You want to leave some of my hair still attached?" he teased. "Or are you collecting it for your scrapbook?"

"I'm sorry." All the fear and sadness she'd been trying to hide rushed up to the surface. Tears surged into her eyes, running down her face to the sofa cushions before she could wipe them away.

"Leah, are you *crying?*" Miguel asked incredulously, nuzzling her face with his own. Her tears wet both their cheeks, making their skin hot and slick. "It's okay. You just pulled a little hard is all. I didn't mean to make a big deal."

"It's not that." Her arms were tight around him again. "It's just . . . It's just that you're not taking this seriously, Miguel. Don't you see? If you insist on staying here to go to college, you're going to force me to leave you. You're splitting us up and you don't even know it!"

Miguel looked stunned. "That's not true."

"It is! College is something I've looked forward to all my life, and you can't even thumb through a few brochures."

Miguel pushed up onto one elbow and stared down at her. "Leah . . . it's just not possible, that's all. Even if finances weren't an issue, you must know it's already too late for me to apply to any of those places."

"No, it isn't. You could still get your application postmarked today if we took it over to the post office. You'd just have to—"

"Have copies of my transcripts and SAT scores. Plus letters of recommendation and a whole bunch of other stuff I don't have. It's too late, Leah."

His words left no room for hope. She felt the tears well up again as she finally admitted he was right.

"Look," he added hurriedly, his tone pleading, "would it really be that awful to go to Clearwater University for a year? I know it's not your dream school, but I also know I can get in there. We could take classes together. And then, after a year, maybe we could transfer. I'd apply anywhere you want."

Yeah, maybe *we could transfer*, Leah thought. And maybe Miguel would have a better chance with a successful first year on his transcript.

But as far as her future was concerned, his plan was an enormous risk. She was never going to be more attractive to the top schools than she was right now. And what if Miguel decided he *liked* CU? Maybe he wouldn't want to transfer. Maybe he'd forget he'd ever promised her he would.

Was she really willing to take that chance?

"So, what are you going to do tomorrow on your big day off?" Jenna teased Caitlin.

To avoid harassment by younger sisters wanting to use the second-floor bathroom, Jenna had temporarily turned her desk into a vanity. A lighted makeup mirror was propped in front of her, and accessories and makeup lay spread out on all sides. Jenna could just see Caitlin in the mirror as she wrapped a section of long brown hair around a hot roller.

"Walk dogs," Caitlin replied exhaustedly from her bed. She was sprawled out on her back. "Dogs, dogs, dogs."

Jenna rotated in her desk chair to better see her tired sister. "You don't exactly look like party material tonight, Cat. Are you sure you can stay awake until midnight?"

Caitlin raised her head slightly, the smile on her face sardonic. "Do I *ever* look like party material? I can't believe I let Mary Beth talk me into this."

"It'll be good for you," Jenna said, glad that Mary Beth had finally come through. The oldest Conrad girl was at yet another friend's house, but she'd promised to be back by eight-thirty to take Caitlin to a New Year's Eve party. "You never do anything fun."

Caitlin groaned and dropped her head to the pillow. "Who said parties were fun?"

Rolling her eyes, Jenna spun back around in her chair to get ready for her date with Peter. She was going to a party too—the open one at Jon Young's house. She and Peter had gone back and forth on whether or not they wanted to attend, but in the end they'd decided to try it. There wasn't anything else for high-school kids to do that night. Besides, all their friends were going to be there.

"So, dinner was fun last night," Jenna said as she clipped her last curler into place.

"Wasn't it?" Caitlin sat up. "Mary Beth was hilarious."

"Yeah, she was. I can't remember when I laughed so hard."

"All those stories about her roommates . . ." Caitlin trailed off, mentally reliving the conversation.

"I know. I was pretty mad at her while we were cooking dinner, but once we sat down at the table, it was like somebody threw a switch or something. Her personality totally changed. I mean, who knew she could be so irresistible?"

"I did," Caitlin said wistfully.

"Well, sure. I did too. I just forgot, that's all."

Caitlin nodded. "Peter got in a few good jokes too."

Jenna felt a smile steal over her face. "Yeah, he did." There was no denying that the evening had been a complete success. The food had been delicious, the company congenial—even Maggie had behaved.

"And what about David?" Jenna asked. "Don't you think he's gotten cute?"

The question had been random, but Caitlin's reaction was quite specific. Her face turned crimson and her mouth dropped open. A moment later it slammed shut, sealed as tightly as a vault.

"Ooh! You do!" Jenna cried excitedly. "You think he's *really* cute!"

The tomatoes in Caitlin's cheeks deepened to the color of beets. She put two fingers to her lips, her brown eyes begging Jenna to keep her voice down. "Shhh! I don't want . . ."

She paused and glanced at their bedroom floor, indicating the two lower stories full of people. "I don't want *everyone* to know."

"Know what? Anyone can look at David and see that he's cute for themselves. It's not that big a deal. Unless you *like* him . . ."

Caitlin's brown eyes went wide with alarm.

"You *do*!" Jenna squealed, unable to believe shy Caitlin had finally fallen for someone. "You *like* him, don't you?"

"Shhh! Shhh! Shhh!" Caitlin hissed, frantically crossing the room. Reaching Jenna's chair, she grabbed it by both arms and leaned close to her sister's face. "You've got to stop saying that," she whispered desperately.

"Why? No one can hear me."

"In this house? Come on." Caitlin glanced toward their closed door as if she expected an army to be lurking on the other side, ears pressed tightly to the wood.

"All right." Jenna relented, lowering her voice. "But you're going to have to give me some details. How long have you liked him?"

Caitlin flinched, then took a deep breath. "Eighth grade."

"Eighth grade!" Jenna shouted, forgetting her bargain. "When you were in eighth grade, he was . . . already a junior in high school!"

"No," Caitlin said quietly, "since *he* was in eighth grade."

Jenna stared, stunned. Caitlin had had a crush on David Altmann since she was in the fifth grade? And never breathed a word of it? "But, Caitlin," she gasped. "Why?"

Caitlin shrugged, her hands still on Jenna's armrests. "He just seems . . . I don't know . . . right." Releasing the chair abruptly, she stood up, blushing again. "You can't tell *anyone* about this, Jenna. Ever. Promise me."

"But, Caitlin—"

"No. Promise." Caitlin's brown eyes pleaded along with her voice.

"Lots of people have crushes." Jenna was stalling, hating the idea of keeping such good news to herself. "We all know about Maggie's crush on Scott Jenner."

"Only because Maggie wanted us to. Besides, that's just a little-girl thing. It'll all blow over the first time someone else asks her out."

Her words gave Jenna a thrill. Caitlin didn't just like David, she was serious about him! And Jenna was the only other person in the entire world who knew.

"Well . . . all right," she said at last, reluctant to be forced into secrecy but feeling undeniably important to have earned Caitlin's trust. "I'll only tell Peter, then."

"Jenna!" Caitlin exclaimed, half frantic. "You can't tell anyone!"

"But . . . not even Peter?"

"*Especially* not Peter! What are you thinking?"

"Oh. Right. Well, what if I just hint around a little? I'll bet I can find out if David likes anyone."

"If you do, I'll make you sorry," Caitlin said so matter-of-factly that Jenna nearly believed she was serious. "Come on, Jenna. I'm not asking for much. Can keeping a secret really be so hard?"

Jenna felt her eyes go a little rounder. Was Caitlin kidding? Keeping *this* secret was going to be torture.

"Woo-ooo! Happy new year!" Cindy White cried through her open window, leaning on the car horn as she pulled up to a stoplight.

Melanie cringed in the backseat and slid down farther between Tanya Jeffries and Angela Maldonado. The guys in the pickup to their left were already checking out the five CCHS cheerleaders wedged into Cindy's new Volkswagen Beetle—it wasn't as if they needed the encouragement.

"New Year's isn't for four more hours," Tanya told Cindy, reading Melanie's mind. "You're starting a little early."

Cindy flashed the guys in the truck her biggest game-day smile. "Just warming up," she said through clenched teeth.

Sue Tilford, Cindy's best friend, leaned across the gearshift to smile at the boys as well. "We're going to a party."

I'll bet they could have guessed that, Melanie thought. The five of them were dressed to kill, in an abundance of black and rhinestones. Only Angela had bucked the trend with a dress of palest pink, a floppy wide ribbon tied into a bow atop her long brown curls. The innocent look really worked for Angela. *Probably because she really is innocent*, Melanie thought with a sigh.

The light changed, and Cindy drove off without a single backward look for her admirers. "So, who's everyone going to hook up with at the party?" she asked. "We ought to make plans now so everyone gets home okay."

"You're driving me," Sue told her immediately. "I don't care if Josh Stockton finally notices you. I don't care if he proposes marriage. You're driving me home or else—"

"Or else someone else will," Cindy concluded with a mischievous smile. "Leave those options open. How about you, Melanie?" she called back over her shoulder. "Got big plans for anyone tonight?"

"No," Melanie answered quickly. A little too quickly, but nobody seemed to notice.

"Tanya?" Cindy asked.

Tanya grinned and tossed her black hair. "I might have my eye on someone."

"Ooh, Tanya!" Angela leaned across Melanie to better see her friend as she, Cindy, and Sue began pumping Tanya for information. Tanya only laughed, deflecting all their questions with deliberately useless hints.

Caught in the middle of the inquisition, Melanie felt a hundred miles away. She smoothed the skirt of her short black dress and took a long, deep breath, relieved to have Tanya temporarily drawing the fire. She had absolutely no intention of telling her friends she'd be looking for Jesse that night.

I just don't need that particular bit of information getting back to Vanessa, that's all. Ever since Jesse had dumped the senior cheerleading captain, any exchanges between her and Melanie had been frigid, at best. *Why antagonize her further when there's nothing going on?*

Yet.

Melanie suddenly realized her hands were sweating. Moving them away from her dress, she nervously adjusted the lapels of her white satin jacket. The whole situation seemed unreal. She couldn't believe she was in a car, on her way to a party, actually looking forward to seeing Jesse Jones.

She wondered where he was at that moment. Was he in a car too? Was he thinking about seeing her? Was he as overdressed as she was?

Was he nervous?

Because I almost feel kind of sick, she thought, leaning forward to get some more air. *And I'm not sure that's such a good sign.*

Five

"Come on, Jeff," Courtney Bell said, pointedly ignoring Nicole. "Let's hurry. It's cold out here."

Grabbing her boyfriend by the arm, she began pulling him up the Youngs' front walkway, leaving Nicole behind. Jeff resisted at first, then—with one last apologetic glance back over his shoulder—allowed himself to be led toward the New Year's party inside.

Even before Courtney reached the front porch, Nicole could hear the booming bass of a cranked-up stereo and the shouts and laughter of Jon's guests. When Jeff opened the door, sound poured out like water, and light shone into the yard. For a moment Nicole made out the bobbing heads of a crowd in the illuminated rectangle of the doorway. Then Courtney slammed the door shut behind them, leaving Nicole outside in the dark.

"Oh, that is *so* immature!" Nicole muttered under her breath, but it was hard to be angry when she still felt so guilty.

Despite every resolution and all her best intentions, Nicole hadn't told Courtney about the California trip until just a few minutes before. She'd procrastinated, and postponed, and then plain chickened out. Not until Courtney and Jeff had picked her up for the party, not until they were all in his car and halfway to the party, had she finally come out with the awful news that she, Jenna, and Melanie been invited to the U.S. Girls finals.

"Hey, congratulations!" Jeff had exclaimed. "When do you girls leave?"

Courtney had taken things less well.

"You're not *going*," she'd said disbelievingly, twisting around in the passenger seat. "Of all the nerve! How could Leah even *think* of inviting Jenna instead of me? And after I sat through that whole stupid thing in St. Louis, too! I hope you told her to take her trip and shove it."

A long, suffocating silence had descended in the car. Nicole could hear herself breathing.

"Nicole?" Courtney had said dangerously.

"Well . . . geez, Court, it's California! And you know how I feel about model—"

"You're not going." This time it was an order. "If you do, you're no friend of mine."

"For Pete's sake, Courtney . . . ," Nicole had begun.

"Don't you think that's a little harsh?" Jeff had asked.

"Yes!" Nicole had exclaimed gratefully.

"Just stay out of this, Jeff."

"Excuse *me*." Jeff had thrown his girlfriend an irritated look.

Courtney never saw it. Her gaze had been fixed on Nicole. "Nicole knows who her friends are. She *used* to, anyway. And if she wants to keep them, she'll do the right thing."

Nicole had known that Courtney expected her to say she wouldn't go, but there was such a thing as asking too much. Besides, it wasn't as if Courtney had anything to *gain* if Nicole stayed home.

So, instead of giving in, Nicole had simply crossed her arms and slid lower in the backseat, hoping that Courtney wouldn't want to make a really huge scene in front of Jeff. Her gamble had paid off. Courtney had stared her down another few seconds, then spun angrily back around without a word.

The thing was, now that they were at the party, Courtney still wasn't speaking to her.

I hate it when she does this, Nicole thought, reaching for the closed front door. Courtney had given her the silent treatment before, of course—lots of times—but it hadn't happened for so long that Nicole had thought she'd outgrown such childishness. Or at least she'd hoped she had.

Inside, the house was already mobbed. Hordes of CCHS students crowded the spacious living room, the girls dressed to the nines and the guys in jeans and sports coats. Purple and silver streamers and balloons decorated the ceiling, the only part of the room Nicole had a clear view of. She could just glimpse a fireplace at one end, though, and a HAPPY NEW YEAR! banner was draped across the pass-through to an adjoining room. Stopping just inside the front door, Nicole rose on her toes to get a better idea of the layout.

"Hi, Nicole. Did you come by yourself?" Jenna asked unexpectedly from beside her, startling Nicole back down to the ground.

Jenna and Peter were standing near the wall, slightly out of the crowd. Jenna's normally straight brown hair was done in soft curls, and the dress she wore was dark blue velvet. Peter just looked like Peter—no matter what he put on, to Nicole he never much changed.

"No, uh, with Courtney," Nicole stammered, horrified by the idea that other people might be thinking the same thing.

Jenna glanced from Nicole, who had just come in, to Courtney and Jeff, already on the far side of the room.

"I, uh, forgot something in the car and had to go back. My, uh . . . my purse," Nicole invented quickly, turning sideways to show Jenna the sleek black bag on her hip. "I told those two to go on without me."

"Are you riding home with them too?" Jenna asked.

Good question. Nicole suddenly realized she might need alternate transportation. Jeff would almost certainly still drive her, but Courtney . . .

"Uh-huh. Do they have any beer?" Nicole blurted out, wincing a moment later when she realized who she had asked.

57

Peter and Jenna exchanged troubled glances.

"They have a lot of alcohol, actually," said Peter. "I didn't know you were a drinker."

"I'm not. Not at all. Well, once in a while. At parties." *Shut up, Nicole! You're only making it worse.* "But, uh, I doubt I'll drink tonight."

The two of them regarded her with dubious expressions.

"Boy, do I need to use the ladies' room!" Nicole exclaimed. It was amazing how little the excuse embarrassed her under the circumstances. "Did you happen to see where it is?"

Jenna pointed over the heads toward the beginning of a hallway on the other side of the room. "Down the hall, then turn right."

"Thanks. I'll see you guys later."

Pushing off through the crowd, Nicole headed for the hallway. As soon as she reached it, though, she realized that the kitchen was just off to her left. And she really didn't need a bathroom—she needed to calm her nerves.

Just one beer, she told herself, heading in that direction.

"Are you having fun?" Peter asked. He had to shout in Jenna's ear to be heard above the music from the nearby speakers.

Jenna nodded. "But I wish . . . Well, I thought people were going to be dancing."

The party had become nearly standing room only—and standing was exactly what everyone was doing. The only activities anyone seemed interested in were talking and drinking, and maybe making out in the upstairs bedrooms. Jenna and Peter had talked to everyone in Eight Prime at various points, as well as to lots of other friends from school, gradually working their way from the living room to the den to the downstairs rumpus room. But now, with two hours still left until midnight, Jenna almost wished they had gone somewhere else.

She glanced at Peter, whose eyes were on the crowd. She had completely forgiven him for going to the homecoming dance with Melanie—but she still hadn't quite gotten over it. She and Peter always had so much fun at dances. She had really hoped that tonight . . .

The song that was playing ended, and a favorite new one began. Peter turned to smile at her. "Want to dance?"

"Here?" She looked doubtfully around the crowded room. "But no one else . . . there's no room . . ."

"They'll make room," Peter said, grabbing her by the hand and pulling her away from the wall. "Come on, Jenna, don't leave me out here dancing by myself." Throwing his body into the music, he motioned for her to join him.

Jenna hesitated a second, embarrassed, then shook her head and began to dance as well. What did she care if other people thought they were weird? They'd still have each other. The thought put a smile on her face that grew with every beat of the music.

As Peter had predicted, people started backing up, leaving a little circle for them to dance in. For maybe thirty seconds, Jenna felt as though the entire room were staring. Then another dancing couple pushed into the circle, smiling as they did, and within a minute nearly everyone was dancing. The few people who chose not to either pressed against the walls or escaped up the stairs, while a steady stream of others pushed past them in the opposite direction, trying to get to the fun. Jenna saw Leah and Miguel come downstairs, hand in hand, and spotted Melanie dancing with Ricky Black.

"I think we started a trend!" Peter laughed.

They danced a second song, then a third. Midway through the fourth, someone opened a pair of windows near the ceiling to let some air into the room. By the sixth, Jenna needed a rest and a cold drink. She and Peter left the dance floor raging behind them and went upstairs to the kitchen.

A cooler of sodas on ice stood open on the floor, a short distance from the keg. Peter reached to the bottom to pull out a couple of ice-cold Cokes. "Do you want to drink these somewhere quieter?" he asked, holding one out to Jenna.

"Let's try the dining room." Ever since the snacks had run out, there hadn't been many people in there, and there weren't any stereo speakers, either.

The dining room turned out to be nearly deserted. Most of the crowd had moved downstairs or was talking in the living room, kitchen, or den. The dining room, off in an awkward corner, had been forgotten by everyone except Peter, Jenna, and two or three other couples who obviously wanted a breather.

Peter pulled out chairs at one end of the table, and he and Jenna sat down with their sodas.

"So. That woke things up," he said with a laugh. "For a minute there, we were the life of the party."

"I'll bet no one even knows we're missing now."

"Give me a minute; then we'll go down and shake things up again."

Jenna smiled and sipped her Coke.

"I wonder what David and your sisters are doing right now," Peter said. "I'm pretty sure Chris and Maura were going to that party too."

In the car on the way to the Youngs' house, Jenna had learned from Peter that the party her sisters were attending was the major college event of the night. She could barely wait to get home and ask Caitlin if she'd known all along that David was going to be there. If so, she had never let on.

"Did, uh, did David plan to meet anyone in particular at the party?" Jenna knew she probably shouldn't ask, but she couldn't see the harm.

Peter gave her a strange look. "Like who?"

"Well, I don't know."

If she asked specifically about girls, it would be a

direct violation of Caitlin's orders. But maybe if she just fished around a little, Peter would catch on and volunteer what she wanted to know.

"An old friend or . . . anyone?"

"I imagine he'll meet a ton of old friends. This is where he grew up."

"Yes, but . . ." *Why is Peter always so dense?* she thought, clenching her teeth in frustration. Anyone else would have *known* she meant a girl.

"But what?"

"But . . . Nothing. Never mind."

This secret was going to kill her.

"Oops! Excuse me," Ben said hastily, backing away from the darkened alcove beneath the staircase. "I just thought . . . I mean, I didn't know . . . uh, sorry." The kissing couple he had just stumbled onto didn't even seem to notice he'd been there as he hurried out of their way.

Stuff like that had been happening all night. Every time he tried to get out of the crowd and find somewhere to watch the party from, someone had already beaten him to it and turned the place into a makeout spot. It was embarrassing.

Worse, it was discouraging.

And as the clock ticked toward midnight, it seemed that more and more of the people at Jon Young's house were pairing off. Even Mark had deserted him to try to romance some girl he knew from chemistry class. "I'll tell you all about it tomorrow," he'd said with a wink before he'd taken off, leaving Ben feeling like the biggest loser on the planet. Not only didn't he have a girl of his own to pursue, he wouldn't know what to do with her if he did.

Ben weaved his way through the crowd again, looking for anyone from Eight Prime. Maybe he could hang out with one of them for a while, or even bum a ride home. He'd seen Nicole in the kitchen earlier. Maybe she was still there.

But although the kitchen was packed, Ben saw no one he knew. The fact that he recognized half the people in the room didn't mean a thing. Everyone knew the people at school who mattered—no one was expected to know a nobody like him. He hesitated at the edge of the white tile floor, wondering if he should go in.

Jon Young was in there, and so was his girlfriend, Brooke. The two of them were dressed like a clothes commercial—up to the minute and cool—and so were the friends who mobbed them, the cooler, and the keg, leaving barely an inch of floor space. Ben looked down at his plain pullover and cords and decided not to venture farther, even before Jon grabbed Brooke, dipped her backward, and kissed her like some old-time movie hero. Brooke's friends screamed with delighted laughter, and somehow an abandoned cup of beer got knocked off the counter in the commotion. Beer splashed the tiles, wetting all the feet and ankles in the vicinity.

"Oh, great!" Brooke exclaimed. "Do you know how much these shoes cost?"

Ben looked down at his own scuffed-up loafers and slunk off in the direction of the living room.

Even before he got there, he heard Dick Clark loud and clear. Someone had turned off the stereo and switched the television to the New Year's Eve broadcast at such a high volume it was painful. The set got turned down just as Ben pushed his way into the room and spotted all the rest of Eight Prime gathered near its big screen.

"Hey, there you guys are!" he shouted, bellowing in his relief. With the television so recently hushed, his voice boomed through the room like a crack of thunder. Heads swiveled his way, and Ben felt his cheeks turn scarlet.

Luckily, Eight Prime barely seemed to notice. Jesse and Melanie cringed a little, but their attention was focused on the television. Miguel had his left arm around Leah's shoulder and his right crossed in front of him to hold her right hand. With her free left hand, Leah clung to the hand on her shoulder, tying the two of them together like some vertical game of Twister. Nicole stood beside Melanie, watching the crowd in Times Square.

"Hi, Ben," Peter said as Ben joined the group.

Jenna flashed him a smile as well. "What happened to Mark?"

Even Peter and Jenna were holding hands that night, something they usually did only when they thought no one was looking.

"He, uh . . . he had something to do," Ben stammered, not caring to go into detail. "So, um, what are you guys doing? Make any resolutions yet?"

Melanie looked up from the TV. "You mean like New Year's resolutions?"

"Yeah."

Leah gazed wistfully at Miguel. "We ought to do that."

"I always make at least one resolution." Jenna's creamy cheeks turned a little pinker as she wrinkled up her nose. "I hardly ever keep them, though."

"Let's all make resolutions this year," Melanie proposed.

Nicole tore her glassy gaze away from the action in Times Square. "Like what?"

"Well . . . I don't know," Melanie said. "But it ought to be something important—something that matters. Come on, you guys, what do you say?"

"Do we have to tell everyone else what it is?" Ben asked apprehensively.

The group had gathered into a circle. Now they searched each other's faces, considering Ben's question.

"No," they all said in unison.

Ben laughed with relief. "Okay, I'll do it, then."

"Me too," Jesse said.

The others nodded, and everyone looked off into space, thinking.

"Don't forget to make it something real," Melanie reminded them.

Jesse rubbed his chin. Nicole closed her eyes. Peter and Jenna smiled at each other, and Leah clung to Miguel as Ben had never seen her do before. Closing his own eyes, Ben focused on Melanie's words.

Something real, he thought, wondering what important change he ought to make in his life.

The answer came to him immediately.

I'm not sure Melanie would think that's important. But his decision was already made. Maybe it was stupid, but he dreaded the thought of his sixteenth birthday in his current unkissed state—he could hear the mocking now. There was no doubt in his mind that people could simply look at him and tell he was a kissing virgin, never mind the other kind.

Let's just work on one thing at a time, he thought, squeezing his eyes shut tighter with embarrassment.

Okay, here goes. I resolve to kiss a girl this year. He opened his eyes, then rapidly shut them again. *On the lips.*

Maybe kissing wasn't that important, but it was absolutely real.

"What time is it?" someone called out on the other side of the crowded living room.

66

Jesse checked his watch, then double-checked it against the digital display being broadcast on the screen: ten minutes until midnight. Half the people in the room were wearing party hats now—goofy paper cones or plastic bowlers for the guys, glitter-encrusted cardboard tiaras for the girls—and curly paper noisemakers were prematurely unfurling in all directions. If he was ever going to make his move, now was the time to do it.

"What a zoo," he said, leaning down to speak into Melanie's ear. Despite the fact that they'd been stuffed into hot rooms for hours, she still smelled so good that for a moment he forgot what he was doing. He hesitated, just breathing. Then Ben's checkered paper noisemaker bonked him in the head, jolting him back to reality.

"Do you want to go outside?" he asked. His voice came out too loud, not at all in the smooth, nonchalant tones he had practiced. Cursing Ben, he hurried to repair the damage. "I mean, it's just so hot in here and—"

"Yes."

"Uh . . . what?"

Melanie turned her head, her eyes meeting his so directly he had to force himself not to flinch. It felt as if she were looking right through him, as if she knew exactly what he was planning.

"Yes," she repeated. "Let's go outside."

"All right!" Too late, he remembered to act cool. "I mean, uh, fine."

Melanie smiled as if she didn't notice his lapse. Or maybe she thought it was cute. Jesse felt his heart beat faster. Was she as into it as he was?

"We're going out to catch some air," he said. Quickly, before the rest of the group could decide to accompany them, he began forcing his way through the crowd to the front door. When his hand touched the doorknob, Jesse finally dared to turn around and make sure Melanie was behind him. She still had a few feet of crowd to get through. He glanced warily back at Eight Prime, hoping they'd all stayed put. No one had followed, but Peter was looking right at him, a strange expression on his face.

Ha! Too bad! Jesse gloated, unable to keep from smiling. *You had your chance, Altmann, and you blew it.* He pulled the door open and gestured Melanie through it with a flourish. *I'm not going to do the same.*

He closed the door, shutting out the party.

Outside, the air was cold, but not nearly as frigid as he had expected. A warming trend had been thawing the town for the last few days, and so far that night temperatures hadn't even hit freezing. In contrast to the stuffy, overheated air inside, the climate on the Youngs' front porch was quite pleasant. Jesse was amazed that no one else was hanging out there, but he supposed they all wanted to see that stupid ball drop in Times Square. Gazing at Melanie in her short black dress and high black heels, he knew he had the better view.

"Are you cold?" he asked.

She shrugged her bare shoulders. "I shouldn't have left my jacket inside."

"Wear my coat," he offered, peeling it off as he spoke.

She hesitated, then stepped toward him, her heels echoing on the wooden boards of the porch. Even though they could still hear the party inside, the outdoor sounds were incredibly sharp, as if the crispness in the air had somehow lent its edge to everything it touched. Jesse reached out to wrap his coat around her, and her light green eyes held his again. Was there a challenge there? An invitation?

She knows, he thought, half nervous, half excited. *She knows, and she's daring me to do it.*

His hands lingered on the front edges of his jacket as he pulled it shut around her. It was a strange sort of power to have her wrapped in his clothes that way, so close he had only to tug to pull her up against him. His breath came faster, and even without his jacket he was barely aware of the cold.

All of a sudden, a commotion sounded inside. "Ten, nine, eight, seven, six, five, four, three, two, one—*happy new year!*"

Noisemakers blared, along with the strains of "Auld Lang Syne." The people who'd had too much to drink began singing with the television, but Jesse had never been more sober. He wasn't taking any chances. Not tonight. Not with this.

"Happy new year," Melanie said softly.

"Happy new year." And then he did give those jacket lapels a tug, pulling Melanie into his arms. His arms went around her, his face lowered to hers. She looked up at him questioningly, as though she knew what would happen, but not how it would turn out. He closed his eyes to shut out their doubts, and a second later his lips met hers, a soft, warm jolt of flesh on flesh.

I'm kissing Melanie Andrews! he thought. More to the point, she was kissing him back. Their lips stayed together, touching, exploring.

But it wasn't the way he had thought it would be. Melanie knew what she was doing. She never talked about it, but he was sure she'd been around. And he'd come a good long way from his first time too. So why did he feel so unsteady? Why were his hands shaking like a kid's playing Spin the Bottle? And why were their kisses so tentative? He had expected this moment to be full of heat and triumph. Instead it was full of . . . he didn't know what.

Lifting his mouth from hers, he searched her face, wondering if she felt it too. There was a glimmer of something in those inscrutable eyes.

"Melanie," he whispered hoarsely, gathering her up until her heels left the ground.

And then he kissed her the way he had meant to the first time.

Six

Melanie was watching the Rose Parade in her living room when her doorbell rang on New Year's Day. Her father hadn't come down from his bedroom yet and, although she'd considered waking him, the possibility that he might be hung over had made her change her mind. He'd already been in bed when she'd come home from the party the night before. If he'd been drinking the New Year in, she really didn't want to know.

Startled by the bell, she scrambled off the sofa to her feet, scuffing her fuzzy slippers across the carpet and then across the marble of the two-story entryway. *It's a good thing I got dressed*, she thought as she reached for the doorknob. Because she already knew who'd be on the other side. There was no doubt in her mind.

"Hi, Jesse," she said, pulling the door open.

He stood there grinning in what he apparently thought was a casual slouch. The pose was as practiced as the rest of his moves. Melanie felt her blood heat up at the thought of the moves he had practiced on her the night before, but if he wanted to act casual, she'd teach him how to act.

"Didja miss me?" he asked cockily.

"Was I supposed to?"

Turning, she walked back into the house, leaving him standing alone at the open door. By the time he had ventured inside, a little of the smirk had been wiped off his face. A little, not all.

"I thought you might, after last night." He took a few steps closer. "Want me to remind you why?"

"My memory's not that bad."

They faced off in the Andrewses' overheated entryway, Jesse trying to read her face, Melanie refusing to let him. If he was looking for weakness, or expecting her to fall all over him . . .

"I got up early this morning and finished my last few hours with Charlie," he said, taking another tack. "Free at last! I thought you might want to help me celebrate."

Removing a paper noisemaker from his coat pocket, he held it out to her with such a hopeful expression that Melanie could feel herself starting to melt. He *was* awfully cute. . . .

So why are you fighting it? You didn't fight it last night.

But she hadn't completely given in either. There had been a few intense minutes out on Jon Young's porch, followed by a single sizzling kiss on her doorstep after she and Jesse had taken home a seriously impaired Nicole. But that was as far as things had gone. That was as far as she'd *let* them go.

Why?

Because I'm still not sure, that's why. How can I be, when one minute he's so sweet and the next he's so conceited? At that very moment, for example, the smile all over his face said he was sure he was irresistible.

I could resist you, Jesse Jones, she told him silently. *I could if I wanted to.*

But why bother?

"Where's the celebration?" she asked, heading toward the closet for a pair of outdoor shoes. "Or is it Charlie who's doing all the celebrating?"

"Very funny," he replied. "It just so happens that Charlie and I are friends now. I might even drop by once in a while to make sure he's okay."

Melanie took out her red wool coat. "Doesn't he have any family at all?"

"It's, uh . . . complicated." Jesse's face clouded, then abruptly brightened again.

"Okay, are you ready to party?" Removing a wad of cardboard and glitter from his other pocket—her hopelessly crushed tiara of the night before—he tried to put it on her head.

"Jesse! Jesse, I am not wearing that!" she protested, laughing and squirming away from him. Her coat dropped to the floor, forgotten in the struggle.

"You wore it last night," he said when she finally

allowed him near her again. "And you looked completely beautiful."

He was serious. So serious she let him put the silly thing on her head. His hands brushed her cheeks as they dropped from her crumpled crown, lingering a second too long for accidental contact. His eyes searched hers for recognition . . . or maybe for permission.

I promised myself I would never, ever get involved with you, she thought, chewing her lip as she met his gaze.

And here she was, getting in deeper by the minute.

She tried not to think about the consequences as she brought the stare-off to the end he'd so obviously hoped for. "So are you going to kiss me, or what?"

"Ooooohhh," Nicole groaned, rolling over in bed. She felt as if her head was being squeezed in a giant nutcracker and her mouth was lined with fuzzy cheese spread. Not to mention her stomach . . .

"Ooohhh," she moaned again as a wave of nausea washed through her. Squeezing her eyes shut against the light seeping in through her curtains, she worried about what time it was.

It's got to be late, she thought, trying to push up from her stomach into a sitting position. Her arms had all the strength of cooked spaghetti. Barely an inch off the mattress, she collapsed facedown into her pillow again. *What was I thinking when I drank all that beer?*

She didn't want to admit that she hadn't been thinking at all. *It was Courtney's fault. If she hadn't been acting so awful . . .*

Her best friend had really outdone herself at the party. Not content simply not to speak to Nicole, she had extended her silent treatment to every member of Eight Prime. Except that with Courtney, there was nothing silent about the silent treatment—it was full of snorts, and *humphs*, and snickers, and other sounds of questionable politeness. Nicole had spent the whole night stressing that her friend was going to come right out and say something nasty to Leah, or—worse yet—to Jenna, and she didn't even want to imagine what. The stale beer in her belly balked now at the mere idea.

By the time twelve-thirty had come around, Nicole was so dizzy from glasses of one-more-beer-and-that's-all-I-really-mean-it that she'd been in no shape to protest when Melanie had noticed her condition and enlisted Jesse to drive her home. The three of them had rolled up her driveway in the BMW as quietly as possible, and Nicole had been relieved to see that most of the house lights were already out. All she had to do was sneak up to her room and sleep it off.

But just inside the entryway, the effects of all those beers had sent her lurching into the antique hall table with the big scalloped mirror on top, and something had crashed to the floor. The sound of shattering glass had exploded through the house, nearly stopping Nicole's heart. For one long, truly awful moment, she'd thought it was the heirloom mirror she'd broken. Then light had flooded the entryway, dazzling her eyes, and Nicole had been confronted by her bathrobe-clad mother.

"My new vase!" she'd cried, pointing to the wet shards of crystal all over the floor. "Nicole, what's the matter with you?"

"Nothing!" Nicole had said quickly, weak with relief at the same sight that had her mother so upset. The vase had been expensive, but it wasn't irreplaceable like the mirror; her mom could buy another one. "I just . . . it was dark . . . and I guess I kind of—"

"I told you not to buy those ridiculous shoes," Mrs. Brewster had snapped. "They were dangerous in the seventies and they're dangerous now."

"Yes. Yes, you did." Nicole seized on the excuse of her new platform shoes like a drowning man seizing a life ring. If her mom found out she'd been drinking . . . "I thought I'd get used to them, but—"

"Just go to bed," Mrs. Brewster had said, exasperated. "I'll take care of this mess myself."

Somehow Nicole had managed to get up the stairs without further incident, the adrenaline of fear temporarily suppressing the alcohol in her bloodstream. But the moment her head had touched the pillow she'd passed out so completely that now it seemed miraculous she'd gotten away without detection. Things could have gone a lot worse.

Except for the way I feel now. That couldn't possibly be any worse.

Determined to rise and shower before her mother got suspicious about how long she'd slept in, Nicole rolled out of bed in one rapid movement. Her thought had been that it would be better to get on her feet quickly, like ripping off a Band-Aid, but a split second later she knew she'd been wrong. The contents of her stomach rose into her throat in a way that made their intentions clear and, despite the fact that her legs were barely cooperating, Nicole raced for the bathroom she shared with Heather. Bursting in through the door on her side of the room, she barely managed to get her head over the toilet bowl in time.

She was sick for only a couple of minutes, the small white room spinning around her. She was still on the floor, just beginning to think about trying to stand, when Heather walked in through the door that adjoined her bedroom.

"Phew!" she exclaimed, holding her nose. "Do you want me to go get Mom?"

"No!" Nicole cried in a panic, struggling to get to her feet. She flushed the toilet hurriedly. "No, don't. That's okay."

"But you're sick."

"No, I'm not. I'm fine." She did feel better, she realized as she switched on the fan and reached for the air freshener. "No point worrying Mom."

Heather watched as Nicole sprayed the room. "Hey, did you sleep in your clothes, or what?" A hard glint of suspicion had entered her gray eyes.

"Huh?" Nicole glanced down at her outfit. Instead of changing into a nightgown before bed, she had apparently settled for the slip she'd worn under her party dress. She hadn't even noticed until Heather pointed it out. "I . . . uh . . ."

"You were drinking!" Heather accused. "That's what that putrid smell is."

"No, I—"

"Just wait till I tell Mom. You are going to be *dead*." Heather turned on her heel and started out of the room.

"No, Heather, wait! Don't tell Mom," Nicole begged.

"Why shouldn't I?"

"Because, well . . . what if she doesn't let me go to California?" Even as she spoke the words, Nicole knew that was exactly what would happen.

"It would serve you right."

"Come on, Heather! I made a mistake. But Mom will make me pay for the rest of my life."

"Oh, well. You should have thought of that before." Heather started walking again.

Nicole could hear her sister crossing her own bedroom on her way to look for their mother. Sprinting to the bathroom doorway Heather had just vacated, Nicole spoke to her sister's back.

"If you don't tell on me, I'll do anything you want," she promised desperately. "Anything. You name it."

Heather hesitated, then stopped. To Nicole it felt like an eternity before she finally turned around, but when she did her eyes glimmered with the beginnings of some sort of deal.

"Anything?" she asked.

The way she said it gave Nicole the shivers. Still, what choice did she have?

"Anything," she repeated. "Just tell me what it is."

Heather smiled. "Well, there is one thing. . . ."

Seven

"**T**his isn't what I want!" Ben muttered to himself, poring over the titles in the self-help section of the bookstore. "I know they've got to have *something* here." For a moment he considered asking for help. Then he came to his senses.

Like I really want to explain what I need to a sales clerk. He blushed at even the thought of such embarrassment.

Frustrated, he walked from aisle to aisle, searching for some other, more pertinent section. Not that he expected there to be a whole *section.* Still . . .

I wouldn't mind if there were.

But no matter where he looked, nothing met his requirements. He was all the way at the back of the store, on the verge of giving up, when his eye caught a flash of hot pink screaming from a bottom shelf.

The Kissing Handbook, a bold white title proclaimed, and beneath that was a pale pink kiss, as if a giant had blotted her lips there.

"Yes!" Ben whispered triumphantly. Looking around to make sure no one was watching, he snatched the small hardbound book from the rack and flipped it over to read the back cover.

WANT TO BE A KILLER KISSER? WITH THE KISSING HANDBOOK, YOU'LL LEARN TRIED-AND-TRUE TECHNIQUES FROM EXPERTS AROUND THE GLOBE.

"Oh, yes," Ben said, not bothering to read any further. A quick flip through the pages convinced him he'd finally found what he'd been looking for: an actual kissing manual.

Quickly shucking off his jacket, he hid the book underneath it and began hurrying toward the front of the store. It wasn't until he was halfway to the register that he realized he couldn't pay for his purchase without showing it to a cashier.

And the only two working that day both happened to be teenage girls.

Great, he thought, feeling sweat break out on the back of his neck as he glanced from one to the other. Not slowing his steps in the slightest, he made an immediate U-turn and headed into the magazine section. *Now what?*

He considered buying the book via the Internet and paying for some type of extra-super-express shipping. But he'd need a credit card for that, and there was no way he wanted his mom in on this little project. Besides, he'd only given himself a year to accomplish his goal. With his track record, he didn't have a moment to lose.

Be a man, he ordered himself sternly. *Get a grip.*

No one's going to say anything to you; they want to sell these books.

Even so, when he finally got in line it was in front of the older of the two cashiers. She looked as though she might be in college, and therefore less likely to blab to anyone at CCHS.

"It's, uh, for my little brother," he fibbed before she even said hello. He tried to look sophisticated as he pushed the book toward her across the counter.

The cashier glanced skeptically from him to the book and back again, and Ben realized his mistake. Of all the colors in the world, why did the cover have to be that particular shade of fuchsia? Wasn't the fact that a person needed to buy such a thing embarrassing enough?

"I mean my sister!" he amended loudly, wishing he'd just kept his big mouth shut. "It's for my little sister."

"Uh-huh," said the cashier, holding out her hand for the money.

By the time he had escaped into the Saturday crowd at the mall, his purchase safely hidden in a plastic shopping bag, Ben's cheeks were as pink as the cover.

I don't care, he told himself as he headed for the bus stop. *I got what I was looking for.*

As soon as he got home, he'd cover *The Kissing Handbook* with a nice brown paper bag. Then he'd memorize it front to back.

That way, when the big moment comes, I'll be completely ready, he thought.

If the big moment ever came.

Ben sighed. *Well, if nothing else, at least I'll be able to fake it in conversations with other guys.*

"This was a mistake," Leah said, emerging from the department store dressing room. "I'm not ready to do this."

"What are you talking about?" Miguel jumped up from the chair where he'd been waiting and hurried over to meet her. "The contest is only two weeks away."

Leah made a face. "I just feel so stupid trying stuff like this on." She gestured impatiently at the floor-length sequined gown she was wearing. "I'm like a little girl playing dress-up. And . . . besides . . . Let's just forget it, all right? I'll come back tomorrow with my mother."

"You don't trust me," he said, looking wounded.

"What? I do too."

"Then let me help you pick the dress. If I can't be with you at the contest, I at least want to know what I'm missing."

Leah rolled her eyes. "You're not missing a darn thing."

"Which only shows what you know." Taking her gently by the shoulders, he turned her around until she faced the three-way mirror. "Look how beautiful you are."

She had to admit that she looked all right. The dress, the first one she'd tried on, was a knockout. It shimmered in a shade of green that reflected in her hazel eyes. But still . . .

"I wish I could go with you," he said, reading her mind.

"I wish it more." Twisting out from under his hands, she put her arms around him and buried her face in the crook of his neck, closing her eyes against the disapproving looks from the saleswoman.

"It's only for three days, and then you'll come back. You *will* come back, right?" he added in a teasing tone.

"Of course," she said sulkily.

"No, but Leah . . ." He pulled away from her embrace to look her in the eyes. "What if you win?"

"What do you mean?"

"We still haven't even figured out the college thing. And if you win this contest . . ." His usually clear brown eyes had clouded. "You know I love you, right? No matter what?"

She nodded, a sudden lump in her throat. "I love you too. So much."

She used to think that was all that mattered. Now it only made things harder.

Brrriiiiing!

Melanie had been expecting Tanya's call, but the loud, sudden noise in the hard-surfaced room still

84

sent her halfway out of her bubble bath. Hastily drying her hands on a thick white towel that lay on the tub's edge, she snatched the cordless phone off the marble ledge where she'd placed it and fumbled with the buttons. "Hello?"

"Hey, gorgeous. Whatcha doing?" Jesse said on the other end.

"Jesse!" For a moment she felt as surprised as if he had walked in on her in person. Her heart pounded, and her bath was suddenly too warm. With her free hand, she made sure the bubbles covered her, no matter how silly that was. There was something about talking to Jesse naked that was incredibly embarrassing.

"Are you washing dishes or something? What's that sound?"

"What sound?" Melanie countered, not wanting him to know that he'd surprised her in the bathtub. At the current stage of their entanglement, that was way too much information. She froze dead in the water, making sure not to cause one more ripple. "I don't hear anything."

"I thought I heard water."

"Must have been something on your end."

"Hmmm," he said finally, dropping it. "So what are you doing? Maybe I'll come over."

"Tonight? I'm going out with Tanya."

"It's Saturday night!"

"I know. That's why we're going out."

There was a significant pause on Jesse's end. "Well,

then, where are you going?" he asked at last. "Maybe I'll stop by there."

Melanie felt a jolt of apprehension. She still didn't even know where things were headed with Jesse, but if he was going to get all clingy on her, they definitely wouldn't go far.

"I don't think that would be fair to Tanya," she said slowly. "And anyway, I just saw you yesterday."

"We went to brunch. Big deal. Besides, I didn't know we were keeping score."

"I'm not. But just because we . . . I still have a life, you know? Whatever this is between us, it doesn't have to move so fast."

"You think this is moving fast? I can move a lot faster."

Melanie rolled her eyes toward the ceiling. If that was supposed to impress her . . .

Jesse seemed to sense his mistake. "Okay, so you're busy tonight. I get the picture."

"Good."

"How about tomorrow?"

Melanie shook her head. He didn't get the picture at all.

Eight

"Why don't you go over there and talk to him?" Jenna urged.

"Shhh!" Caitlin replied, turning crimson. "Stop it, Jenna."

"Stop what?"

"You know what." Her sister cast an embarrassed glance toward the edge of the church parking lot, where David Altmann was talking to Peter, Mary Beth, and a couple of other people who had attended the early service.

"He's leaving for school right from here, you know. This could be your last chance."

Caitlin gave her an incredulous look and turned away.

What's the big deal? Jenna thought, frustrated. *I'm not saying to run up and kiss him, but could it hurt to say good-bye?*

Ever since the New Year's Eve conversation where Jenna had discovered her sister's crush, Caitlin had completely clammed up about David. The couple of times Jenna had tried to force her to talk, she'd made rapid excuses and left the room. Mary Beth was the one who'd revealed, during dinner on New Year's day, that she and Caitlin had spent most of their time at the party the previous night hanging out with David and his old high-school friends. However, her casual tone had made it clear she didn't know Caitlin's secret.

I almost wish I didn't know either, Jenna grumbled to herself. *It's bad enough that I can't tell anyone—now even Caitlin won't talk about it.*

"Are you girls ready to go home?" Mrs. Conrad said, walking over to join them near Jenna's favorite bench. Maggie, Allison, and Sarah followed at her heels. "Where's your father?"

"Talking to Mr. Chapman." Jenna pointed toward the entrance to the church, where a fairly large group had gathered.

A slightly anxious look drew her mother's brows together. "He knows Mary Beth is in a hurry to get home so she can leave for school."

As if to emphasize the point, Mary Beth looked over just then and spotted them all together. Waving, she hurried toward them, bringing David and Peter along with her.

"So! It looks like this is good-bye," David said cheerily, smiling as he walked up. He was wearing an Irish fisherman's sweater that made him stand out in that sea of coats. "I'm leaving for school in just a few minutes. My parents are driving me straight to the station from here."

Mary Beth raised her eyebrows at her mother, clearly trying to remind her that she was dying to be on her way as well. "What's keeping Dad?"

"I'll go get him in a minute," Mrs. Conrad said. "It was so nice seeing you again, David. College is obviously agreeing with you."

David seemed embarrassed by the compliment. His cheeks turned pink while his blue eyes wandered off. "Thanks, but graduating will agree with me more. I'm ready for real life to start anytime."

Mary Beth laughed. "Aren't we all! Speaking of which, I'm going to get Dad myself or we'll never get out of here. See you around, David. Maybe I'll catch you again this summer. Or are you going to live somewhere else after graduation?"

David shrugged. "I'll have to find out where I'm working first. I haven't planned that far ahead."

"Okay. Well, have a good trip back." Mary Beth tossed him a wave and was off, her auburn curls bouncing in time to her walk.

"Bye, Mary Beth!" Peter called to her back. "See you soon."

She wiggled her fingers over one shoulder without turning around.

"I guess we're out of here too," David told the

group, glancing toward the Altmanns' car in the corner of the parking lot. His parents were both standing beside it now, looking around for their sons. "Good-bye, Caitlin. It was fun dancing with you the other night."

"You *danced?*" Maggie exclaimed disbelievingly, turning to her sister.

Caitlin blushed, but David was already walking away, off toward the parking lot.

"I'll call you later," Peter told Jenna. "Sometime this afternoon."

Jenna nodded distractedly as he left. All her attention was focused on David and Caitlin.

"Go after him," she whispered, nudging her sister in the ribs. "Who knows how long it'll be before you see him again? Ask him to give you a call sometime."

Caitlin stared as if Jenna had lost her mind, then turned and walked off toward the family's van, which was parked on the opposite side of the lot from the Altmanns' car. Her actions left Jenna sighing.

If only Caitlin could be more like Mary Beth once in a while! she thought, leaving her mother and younger sisters behind as she hurried to catch up with Caitlin. *Not all the time, of course. Just when it would do her some good.*

"Well, maybe he'll come home for Easter," she whispered consolingly as she reached Caitlin's side. "You never know—he might."

Caitlin shook off her sympathy. "It's okay, Jenna. I'm fine." She turned and smiled so Jenna could see for herself.

She looked better than fine, actually. Jenna couldn't imagine what had suddenly put such a smile on her sister's face. Unless . . .

Unless it was David saying he'd liked dancing with her. Could she really be satisfied with that little bit of attention?

Jenna snuck another look. If anyone could be satisfied with so little, it was Caitlin. The realization made Jenna determined to help her sister get more.

But how?

If only I could talk to Peter! she thought as she and Caitlin climbed into the Conrads' big van. *I could find out if David likes Caitlin. Or at least if he likes someone else.*

Jenna sighed again. *Why, why, why did I ever promise Cat I'd keep this secret?*

Jesse checked the digital clock on his dashboard as he pulled into the Andrewses' driveway: 2:06.

He parked, then climbed out of the car and stared up at the huge glass-and-concrete mansion in front of him, looking for some sort of clue. *I hope she's home,* he thought, a little nervously. He hadn't actually told Melanie he was coming.

Well, I shouldn't have to. What's the big deal if I drop

by once in a while? This whole town's in a coma on Sundays anyway—she ought to be glad to see me.

Still, he remembered what she'd said the night before about not moving things so fast, and his feet hesitated halfway to her front door. Maybe he should play things cooler. Maybe he should wait for her to come to him.

Except that waiting was driving him crazy. He'd known he wanted Melanie since practically the first time he'd seen her. And now that he'd felt his arms around her, now that he'd actually kissed her, she was all he could think about. He wondered what she was doing every minute of every day, and at night he saw her face when he closed his eyes. He even dreamed about her. She had taken over his thoughts completely, to the point where he didn't feel in control anymore.

And that's why I have to see her, he decided, walking the last few steps to her door. *If I let her start running things now . . .*

He punched her doorbell decisively, his doubts cleared away. He would do a lot of things for Melanie, but he was still the man in this relationship.

At last Melanie answered the door, wearing faded jeans and a checkered apron over a tank top. Her usually perfect blond hair was tucked, unstyled, behind her ears, and a smudge of flour powdered one cheek.

"Jesse! What are you doing here?" she exclaimed.

"I'm glad to see you too," he returned, determined

not to let her rattle him. "But you didn't have to get dressed up for me."

Melanie's green eyes narrowed. "When you drop in on people, you can't expect miracles. You're lucky I'm dressed at all."

"Or not," he said, imagining a whole range of possibilities.

"Put your hormones on hold, Jones. Amy's in the kitchen."

"Amy?" Jesse couldn't hide his disappointment. "What's she doing here?"

"Strangely enough, I *invited* her. I'm baby-sitting this afternoon."

"You didn't say anything last night about baby-sitting!"

The look she gave him said more than words.

"Well, you could at least have *mentioned* it," he heard himself whining like the world's biggest wimp.

"If you want to help make cookies, come on in. Otherwise . . ."

"Okay, fine. I'll make cookies," he said grumpily.

She finally smiled at him, then turned and walked toward the kitchen. He followed, peeling layers of clothing off his torso as he went.

No wonder she's wearing a tank top, he thought. *Compared to the weather outside, this place feels like the tropics.* He wondered if maybe their heater was broken—stuck on high or something—but he didn't want to push his luck by asking.

In the kitchen, Amy sat perched on the edge of a counter beside a bowl of dough and a half-filled cookie sheet.

"Hi, Jesse!" she called excitedly when she saw him. "Me and Melanie are making cookies!"

"So I hear," he replied, walking over to join her. "Do you think she knows what she's doing?"

"Come taste!" Amy offered earnestly, sticking her finger into the dough and holding it out to him.

"Uh . . . maybe I'll just wait until that's cooked."

"Amy, we're not supposed to put our fingers in the dough, remember?" Melanie chided. "It's not clean for other people that way."

"Oh. Right." Amy looked downcast a moment. Then she popped her finger into her mouth and sucked off every trace. "All clean!" she announced happily, holding it up for inspection.

Melanie laughed. "Um, yeah. Except maybe you should wash your hands again anyway."

"Aw, Melanie," Amy complained as Melanie lifted her off the counter and held her over the kitchen sink, "I just *did* this!"

Moving to the other side of the counter, Jesse sank onto a barstool with a good view of the action. "Hey, do you have any Coke in this restaurant?"

"Just a minute," Melanie said. She got Amy washed up and back into position on the counter, letting her work on putting dough on the sheets with two spoons. Then Melanie opened the big steel refrigerator and found a soda for Jesse.

"Here you go," she said, bringing it around the counter to him instead of just passing it across. Her body brushed into his back as she put it down, and he knew she was flirting. Immediately his arms went out behind him, trapping her in a low reverse embrace that Amy couldn't see.

Melanie wriggled, laughing, but not hard enough to get away. "I have to make cookies," she told him, her voice full of mock reproach.

"Amy's got things under control."

The little girl glanced up at the sound of her name, then looked curiously from one to the other, not fooled by the way they had frozen in place.

"Is Jesse your boyfriend now, Melanie?" she asked with disarming directness.

"No," Melanie said immediately.

But her answer was too rushed, too defensive, and Jesse saw right through it. He tightened his grip, pulling her closer against his back. Melanie didn't resist.

She's just saying that for Amy, he thought, knowing how much she hated to give herself away. *The next time I get her alone, it will be a whole different story.*

Nine

From the desk of Principal Kelly
(Teachers: Please read in homeroom.)

Welcome back, students!

I hope you're as excited as I am to be starting a new semester. The coming months here at CCHS promise to be filled with exciting activities, and I'd like to encourage everyone to take advantage of this fresh start to try a few new things. Branch out and get involved!

This Friday, our basketball team battles it out with the Mavericks in the Mapleton gym at seven o'clock. Even if you can't go to the game, be sure to show the team and everyone else your school spirit by wearing green and gold on Friday.

Also, it's to be expected that a certain amount of confusion may accompany the finding of new classrooms today. Teachers are therefore asked to use their judgment in writing tardies. Tomorrow, however, feel free to write away.

Go, Wildcats!

"I can't believe vacation is already over," Liz Hartman whined in the cafeteria on Monday. "And my mom didn't let me do anything good. What did you do, Nicole? Did you go anywhere? Did you go to the party at Jon's house?"

Nicole smiled weakly from the other side of the table. When she'd spotted Liz sitting over by the wall, an empty seat across from her, it had seemed like a gift. Courtney still wasn't speaking to her, and Nicole wasn't in any hurry to seek out Eight Prime after the way she'd embarrassed herself on New Year's Eve. All she'd wanted to do was find an inconspicuous place to sit with someone she knew well enough to talk to, so she didn't look like too much of a loser. Unfortunately, all Liz wanted to do was ask personal questions.

"I, uh, I did a few things," Nicole said vaguely, not about to admit that her parents had sent her to Bible school the whole first week. "I was at the party for a while. It was all right."

At least she hoped it had been all right. The details were a little fuzzy, and she was still praying she hadn't done anything really noticeably stupid as a result of all those beers—besides looking dumb in front of her friends and feeling terrible all the next day, that was.

"I heard it was fantastic!" Liz exclaimed, peering at Nicole as if they must be discussing different events. "Everyone else said . . ."

Nicole tuned Liz out as she ran through her second-hand version of Jon's party, regurgitating everything from the number of people who had attended to the color of Brooke Henderson's dress. The fact that Nicole had been there and must have seen everything Liz was describing didn't deter her in the slightest. Nicole tried to keep her expression interested, but her thoughts were far away.

She wondered if Courtney was somewhere in the crowded cafeteria behind her, and how long they were going to fight. It killed her to have her best friend mad at her, and Courtney had to know that. Why couldn't she just be happy for her like everybody else?

Because it really isn't fair, Nicole had to admit. *Sure, it's Leah's right to invite who she likes, but Courtney was there for her at the preliminaries and Jenna didn't even come. No wonder Court thinks she should be the one going to California.*

Nicole stabbed at the congealed apple crisp on her tray, not about to eat it. *Well, actually she was there for me, not Leah. But the end result was the same, wasn't it?* She knew that in Courtney's mind it was, anyway.

"And *then* I heard that Josh Stockton and Cindy White . . . ," Liz went on excitedly.

Normally Nicole would have been fascinated by any type of gossip involving a cheerleader, but there was so much else on her mind that day.

Like that stupid bargain I made with Heather, she thought worriedly. *Not that I had any choice about that.* She never should have let herself get into such a vulnerable position. But she had, and now the little creep owned her. There was no way out except to—

"Nicole!" Courtney's voice cried behind her. "Nicole, I've been looking for you everywhere!"

Nicole spun around on the bench, unable to believe her ears. "You have?"

But her first good look at her friend told her something was very wrong. Courtney's pale skin was flushed a deep, blotchy pink, and her eyes were swollen and wet. Her red hair frizzed around a face that was nothing short of tragic.

"Court, what's the matter?" Nicole gasped.

Courtney answered by grabbing her by the wrist and pulling her to her feet. "I need to talk to you. Come on, let's go to the library."

Nicole reached down to retrieve her backpack. "Sorry, Liz, but I have to go."

"What about your lunch?" Liz protested. "You barely even ate."

Courtney glanced at the tray. "Were you going to?"

Nicole shook her head, and Courtney dragged her off without another word.

They never made it to the library. Halfway down the hall, Courtney started crying, and Nicole pulled her into the nearest bathroom. Courtney checked the stalls to make sure they were alone, then began to cry in earnest.

"Jeff broke up with me!" she wailed. "Can you believe it?"

"But . . . why?" Nicole asked, shocked.

"I don't even know. I don't understand it." Tears poured down Courtney's cheeks, further reddening her eyes. She didn't bother to wipe them away as she looked to Nicole for answers. "He says we have nothing in common, but so what? We've *never* had anything in common."

"I—I don't know what to say," Nicole stammered truthfully.

But even as she reached to hug her friend, her mind was digging out a dozen little signs that things between Courtney and Jeff hadn't been going too well for a while. They had totally different personalities, for one thing. More importantly, they had totally different values. Nicole remembered how disappointed Courtney had been when Jeff wanted to work at Eight Prime's charity haunted house instead of going to the big open party, for instance, and what a hard time she'd given him about his friendship with overtly religious Guy Vaughn—not to mention Peter and Jenna, who she *still* didn't cut any slack. And there were always little arguments, like Jeff telling Courtney she was sarcastic, or Courtney telling Jeff to stay out of her fight with Nicole.

It was inevitable, Nicole realized, rubbing her friend's back. *I should have seen it coming.*

And since it had been coming anyway, how lucky for Nicole that it had happened when it did. The timing couldn't be better to get Courtney's mind off the California trip.

"I am so sorry, Court," she soothed, completely sincere in her sympathy yet equally full of relief. "I know how you must feel."

Courtney sobbed brokenheartedly into her shoulder. "I knew you would. I had to find you, Nicole."

Nicole smoothed Courtney's curly hair. "I can't stand fighting with you."

"Me—Me either." Courtney raised her tear-streaked face. "You know what? This is good. We've hardly spent any time together ever since I met Jeff. But now that you're not so busy with the God Squad and I'm . . ." She hesitated, her face threatening to crumple again; then she took a deep breath and went on. "Well, we'll just have to do *everything* together now, that's all."

Nicole couldn't hold back her smile. She was forgiven!

"I'd like that. I really would."

"It'll be just like the old days," Courtney declared, wiping her face on her sweater sleeve. "We'll eat lunch together every day."

"Call each other every night?"

"And hang out together all weekend." Letting go of Nicole, Courtney pushed her way into the nearest stall and grabbed a length of tissue to blow her nose. "Who needs men?"

"No kidding!" Nicole agreed. After her disasters with Jesse and Guy, she'd be happy to give dating a rest.

"Good, so it's settled then. When are you going to call Leah?"

"Huh?"

"About the trip," Courtney said, looking at her with disbelief. "You're not going to California *now*. Right?"

Uh-oh, Nicole thought as the ugly truth finally hit her. Courtney hadn't forgiven her for wanting to go to California. *She just assumes I'll stay home now and spend my time comforting her instead.*

Nicole swallowed hard.

That wasn't going to happen.

"You should have been there, Ben," Mark bragged. "Not that I missed you or anything."

"No. Of course not," Ben said miserably, too depressed even to eat his Jell-O. Mark had been filling him in on the details of his hot New Year's Eve make-out session with Candice Barns, the girl from his chemistry class, ever since lunch had started.

"So, did *you*, uh, score with anyone?" Mark asked. Ben squirmed on the hard cafeteria bench. "At the party? Nah, all my friends were there. I . . . I was busy."

Mark's face was skeptical. "Your loss, man. You can see your friends anytime."

Ben didn't know what to say. When he'd met Mark, he'd thought they had a lot in common. But now . . .

"Hi, Ben. Do you have a minute?" a sweet voice asked behind him.

Ben would have said yes to anyone at that point, but when he turned around and saw Angela he jumped to his feet, nearly tripping himself in his rush to extricate his legs from the crack between the table and the immovable bench.

"Sure, Angela. What's up?"

Angela dropped into the seat he'd just vacated and pushed his mostly empty tray out of the way. "Oops, were you done with that?" she asked, glancing back over her shoulder at him with an apologetic smile.

"Yeah. No problem."

She slapped a piece of notebook paper onto the place his tray had occupied and pulled a pencil from over one ear, where it had been hidden in her dark brown curls.

"It's math," she said, pointing to the unsolved quadratic equation penciled in at the top of the page. "This new algebra teacher I have is awful! He doesn't explain anything. I asked a couple of people in my class, but they didn't get it either. I mean, I'm not dumb. *Someone* ought to be able to explain this so it makes sense."

She twisted around and gazed up at him hopefully. "I thought that maybe, since you're so good with computers . . . well, I was hoping you might be good at math, too."

"Math?" Ben said blankly, fixated on the beauty mark beside her full lips.

Angela gave him a quizzical look.

"I mean, yeah! Math!" he repeated, snapping out of it. "It just so happens I'm *great* at math."

"Gee, Ben, don't brag or anything," said Mark.

Angela glanced at him, then back at Ben. "Can you believe it's our first day back from vacation and I have a quiz on this stuff on Wednesday? I'm already totally stressing." She put her pencil point down on the problem. "Please tell me you know how to do this."

Ben leaned over her shoulder a little, to make sure he wasn't missing something. No, it was a straight quadratic—as easy as it looked. "Sure, I can do that. Piece of cake."

"But can you explain it to me?" Angela asked, a desperate note creeping into her voice. "I mean it, Ben. I'll be totally grateful."

"Sure. Do you, uh . . . do you want to let me have the pencil?" He bent down further, turning his body sideways to avoid bumping into her as he reached to write on her paper.

"The first thing you have to do is factor it out," he said, trying to ignore how good her hair smelled. "Instead of three x squared plus x minus ten equals zero, you have to turn it into this."

He wrote the next step on her paper:

$$(3x - 5)(x + 2) = 0$$

"Okay, now that's what I don't get. How did you do that?"

Ben turned his head to explain and suddenly found his face only inches from hers. Some advice from *The Kissing Handbook* popped into his head:

The Latin Liplock begins aggressively, with strong lip pressure and a half-open mouth. With one hand, hold your partner firmly by the back of the neck and—

"Ben?"

"Huh? Oh, uh, right," he stammered.

As if he would dare to try something like that on Angela!

"I'm home!" Jenna called, slamming her front door early Monday evening.

"I'm right here. You don't have to shout." Her mother wandered into the entryway, a Christmas garland in her hands. "I'm putting away the last of these decorations."

Jenna nodded, then sniffed the air. "Mmm, what's for dinner?"

"Chili and corn bread. And since you're here, how about giving me a hand? You hold the bag open and I'll stuff it."

Dropping her backpack on the floor, Jenna walked over and picked up the plastic storage bag.

"So, did Chris get the bus dropped off all right?" her mother asked as she wrestled with the garland. "Is everything okay with that?"

Jenna and Peter had met Chris Hobart after school, and the three of them had taken the Junior Explorers' bus to Signs of the Times to have Kurt's name painted on it. "Yep. It's supposed to be ready Saturday. I can't wait!"

"You kids had enough money, then?"

Jenna shook her head. "We would have if we hadn't bought all that sports equipment. We were only a little short, though, so the sign people gave us a discount. Sort of like a donation."

"Nice." Mrs. Conrad climbed a few stairs and began unwinding the next garland from the banister.

"Yeah, except that now we're totally broke. We're going to have to do some sort of fund-raiser as soon as we get back from California." Jenna took a deep breath. "Uh, speaking of California, did you finish checking whatever it was that, uh . . . you know?"

When Jenna's parents had given their permission for her to go on the trip, it had been contingent upon all the arrangements checking out to their satisfaction. Jenna had assumed checking would be a formality, but her mom had turned it into a science. First she had called U.S. Girls directly to get a detailed itinerary. Then she'd called the airlines, confirming the ticket reservations right down to the seat assignments. That Monday Mrs. Conrad had planned to call the hotel where the girls would be staying—the last missing piece of the puzzle.

"Yes, as a matter of fact, I did." Mrs. Conrad freed the garland she'd been working on and came down to put it into the bag Jenna still held. "Everything looks good to me. I don't see any reason why you can't go."

"Thank you!" Jenna exclaimed, both excited and relieved.

"And guess what? I spoke to a manager at your hotel, and they're completely full that weekend with some nationwide Christian youth rally. I guess the U.S. Girls contest is nothing compared to the number of people who'll be there for that. Kids are coming in from all over the country."

"You're kidding. How big is this hotel?"

"Huge. They're holding all their events there too. Except for the big concert. That's at a theater down the block."

"What concert?"

Mrs. Conrad smiled apologetically and shook her head. "It's a Christian rock band; that's all I remember. Fire . . . ? Fire something, I think."

"Fire & Water?" Jenna gasped. "Mom, was it Fire & Water?"

"Maybe. I guess I should have written it down."

"We have to call the hotel and find out!" Jenna dropped the garland bag, ready to run to the phone. "Where's the phone number?"

"Hold your horses, Jenna—we're not making any more unnecessary toll calls. Besides, I already telephoned the conference organizers and they're sending us a brochure. I'm sure it will say who the band is in there. And if it turns out there are times when Leah needs to do things without you, maybe you'll want to go to a few other events too."

"But . . . when's that information coming? If they're selling tickets, they're going to sell out."

Jenna had only discovered Fire & Water's debut CD a couple of weeks before, but it was practically all she had listened to since. There was something about their lyrics that made her want to hear them over and over. She couldn't imagine anything more awesome than seeing the band in concert.

"They said they'd mail it today, so it ought to be here soon. Don't forget that you're there as Leah's guest, though, so her activities come first. For all we know, the concert is on the same night as Leah's big contest."

"That would be terrible," Jenna groaned. Obviously her priority was to be there for Leah, but how could she miss Fire & Water if they were playing down the street?

Jenna imagined herself sitting in the audience at

the modeling finals, waiting through contestant after contestant, all the while knowing that the concert was going on, practically within earshot. It would be like the kind of medieval torture where they pulled people into two pieces. She wanted to see Leah compete and, hopefully, win. But Fire & Water . . .

There's got to be some way to do both, she thought desperately. *There's a way, and I'm going to find it!*

Ten

"I'm sorry, all right?" Leah said. "I didn't know it was such a big deal."

Miguel gave her a sulky look from the driver's seat before fixing his attention on the nasty weather pounding his windshield. Leah had followed him out to the CCHS student parking lot, intending to see him off on his first afternoon at his new job, but a sudden freezing drizzle had temporarily forced them into his parked car.

"You did too," he accused. "I told you I wanted to help pick the dress."

Leah took a deep breath, trying hard not to lose her temper. "My mom would have had to come to the store to pay for it anyway, and . . . I just don't get why you care so much." It even seemed kind of weird to her, actually, that he was suddenly so interested in shopping for women's clothes. "If you want to see it so badly, you can come over anytime."

"That's not the point."

"Then what *is* the point, Miguel?" she asked, exasperated. "Don't we have enough real problems already without making up new ones?"

He shot her a wounded look, then checked his watch. "I have to go. I'll drive you to your car."

"No, wait." Leah's hand reached out to keep him from turning the key. "You can't go like this."

"If I don't, I'll be late."

She knew he was right, but she hated to let him go. She hated that he *wanted* to go when they could be spending the rest of their Tuesday together. And she especially hated to let him leave in the middle of an argument. But what choice did she have?

"Will you at least call me tonight?"

He shrugged. "Maybe."

Just stop it! she wanted to shout. *Why are you being such a baby?*

His brooding reminded her of how impossible he'd been when she'd first met him, and it infuriated her to see him slip back into that old behavior. At the same time, though, she understood what was happening. Not talking was Miguel's way of protecting himself when he thought he was about to get hurt.

Except that this time we're both about to get hurt.

She closed her mind to that line of thinking, refusing to remember college or the demands on her time if she won the U.S. Girls contest. No wonder Miguel was nervous—she was nervous too.

"I wish you didn't have to go," she sighed.

"Well, I do. *Some* of us have to work."

"Oh, don't try to make me feel guilty. You *wanted* this job, Miguel. You were all excited about it."

When he finally looked at her, his expression was cold and distant. "Do you want a ride to your car? Or are you going to walk?"

Ben was on his way to the bus stop Wednesday when he heard footsteps on the sidewalk behind him. "Ben! Ben, wait!" a familiar voice cried.

His heart pumped faster. The voice belonged to Angela.

"Why are you still at school so late?" he asked as she ran up to join him. She was wearing a nylon running suit in the school colors of green and gold, a white ribbon tied around her long ponytail.

"Cheerleading practice. How about you?"

"I was, uh . . . working on something in the library." Even with the brown paper cover he'd put on his kissing handbook, Ben didn't dare risk reading it at home. His mother might get curious.

"I got an eighty-five on my math quiz today."

"Angela, that's great!"

She nodded. "Only three people did better."

"See?" Ben smiled. "I knew you were worried for no reason."

"Are you kidding? You totally saved me. I could kiss you!"

"You could?" For a moment the world closed

down to a tiny little place, with him and Angela suspended at the exact center. The school grounds were mostly deserted anyway, and traffic on the nearby street was light. "Go ahead," he said hopefully.

Angela laughed with astonishment. "Ben, I wasn't . . . that's just an expression."

"Oh."

He'd known that, of course. How could he have said something so stupid, and to Angela, of all people? She was going to think he was completely desperate. Which she probably already did. *But now she's going to know it. Way to not leave any doubt, you jerk.*

And then a miracle happened.

With a shy look around to make sure they were unobserved, Angela leaned over to kiss his cheek. Ben realized what she was doing only an instant before her lips made contact. Ninety percent of him froze where he stood, but one little part of his brain was still alert enough to make a decision, and that was the part that turned his head and told him to pucker up. His sudden, unexpected movement made Angela's kiss land just off the corner of his mouth.

She kissed me! he thought triumphantly, so thrilled he could barely breathe. Maybe she hadn't exactly intended to, but there was no disputing that one little part of Angela's upper lip had touched the far left corners of both of his. He'd done it! He'd snagged his first kiss!

Angela backed up, laughing. "Sneaky, Ben. You almost caught me."

No, I did! I did catch you, he wanted to shout.

But then he realized that Angela's way was better. They didn't have to say it out loud—it was enough that they both knew it.

My first kiss was with Angela Maldonado, he thought, full of pride and relief.

Firsts just didn't get any better than that.

"Are we doing this, or what?" Nicole asked irritably, fidgeting in the driver's seat of her father's Honda. "If we are, then let's get going."

Heather checked her watch, then looked toward the brightly lit entrance of the local grocery store. Although business wasn't as brisk as when they'd first arrived and parked in a quiet corner, there were still people running in and out. The rain of earlier that evening had cleared away, leaving the night sky starry and clear, and the shallow puddles on the pavement were turning to ice.

"It's pretty early," Heather said doubtfully. "We want to be sure they're all asleep."

"At this rate, *I'm* going to be asleep." Nicole yanked the lever to recline her seat and closed her eyes.

This is the dumbest thing I ever let Heather talk me into, she thought resentfully. *And if she was capable of minding her own business, I wouldn't even be here.*

But what choice did she have when her sister was holding all the cards? The tale the little creep could tell was more than enough to get Nicole grounded from the California trip. *Heck, it's probably enough to get me grounded for life.*

So instead of being safe at home that Wednesday night, she was loitering in a grocery store parking lot, dressed all in black and feeling like a total idiot. And it wasn't as if she didn't have other, better things to do. Right then she could have been on the phone with Courtney, listening to her friend rehash every detail of her breakup with Jeff and all the while rearranging the contents of her new suitcase.

Because, so far, she and Courtney were still speaking. On Monday, when Courtney had put her on the spot about the California trip, Nicole had cleverly managed to change the subject without promising her a thing.

I'll tell her soon.

The prospect wasn't even that scary anymore. Anything was better than hanging around a dismal parking lot, waiting for Heather to decide it was time to—

"Okay, let's go," Heather announced.

"*Now?* One minute ago you said it was too early."

"Yeah, but I just thought of something—what if the grocery store closes? We'd better do this part now."

Nicole started to argue, then changed her mind

and jerked her seat upright again. If she couldn't be excused from this stupidity, she might as well get it over with. "Whatever."

Heather threw her door open and started to bolt from the car.

"Wait!" Nicole snapped. "Do you think you could possibly act normal? And take off that stupid hat. You look like a burglar."

Heather shot her a dirty look, then peeled off her black knit cap and tossed it into the passenger seat. Her blond hair gleamed in the darkness. "Satisfied?"

She started walking toward the grocery store, leaving Nicole no choice but to follow.

Nicole had tried to beg off from this part, arguing that it didn't take both of them, but Heather had been adamant. "You're coming, you're paying, and that's that," she'd said. Power had gone straight to her head.

Now she hurried across the parking lot in her black jeans and turtleneck sweater, sweeping her eyes back and forth like the leader of some warped SWAT team. Nicole trailed way behind her, trying to pretend she was alone.

Inside the grocery store, however, Heather wouldn't allow so much distance. She insisted that Nicole stick to her side, the two of them practically joined at the hip all the way to the paper goods aisle. When they turned the last corner and discovered that the aisle was empty, Nicole almost cheered with relief. But instead of taking advantage of their good fortune and grabbing something fast, Heather stood pondering the selection, comparison shopping as if she were spending her own money.

"Hurry up," Nicole whispered, feeling totally conspicuous in the glare of the overhead lights. The linoleum was so shiny she could see her own stressed-out reflection. "Just get some, for crying out loud."

"I think we should use double rolls," Heather said thoughtfully, as if she were deciding a matter of national importance. "The double rolls have twice as much."

"Fine. Get doubles. Get *triples*, I don't care. Let's just get out of here."

Heather turned to stare at her, her gray eyes round. "Do they *make* triples?" she asked seriously.

Nicole had to clench her teeth to keep from screaming. "Here," she said, shoving a plastic-wrapped package of twelve double rolls into Heather's arms. "This is what you're getting. Now, let's go."

Heather started to walk, then stopped. "What about you?"

"What *about* me?"

"You get one too," Heather ordered, pointing back toward the shelf.

"Twenty-four double rolls? That's like forty-eight . . ." Nicole trailed off at the sight of the dead-stubborn look on her sister's face. "You know what? Fine again. I don't even care anymore."

117

Grabbing a duplicate package of toilet paper, Nicole pushed past Heather and headed for the register.

By the time she got in line, she was sweating despite the cold weather. What if someone asked her what she needed so much paper for? Or what if the answer was obvious? What if they took one look and called Security?

I should buy something else—a whole bunch of other stuff to confuse them. Glancing quickly behind her, she realized it was too late. Heather was hard on her heels, and behind her a tired-looking woman with an overflowing cart trapped them both in the checkout aisle.

"Paper or plastic?" the cashier asked, reaching for Nicole's purchase.

"Huh?" Nicole jumped nervously at the mention of paper. "Oh, uh, paper bags are good." *Good and opaque*, she thought.

The elderly cashier peered at her through her granny glasses, as if trying to discover what had made her so jumpy. "All right, dear," she said, ringing up the tissue.

Nicole paid hurriedly, nearly snatching the brown paper bags from the cashier's hands in her eagerness to escape. At last she and Heather were walking back through the icy parking lot on the way to their father's Honda.

"Well, that's the first part over, anyway," Nicole muttered.

"Geez. Don't be such a wimp, Nicole."

It's easy to be brave when you have nothing to lose, Nicole thought sullenly.

And, sure enough, in the car driving down the darkened residential streets, Heather was more excited than nervous.

"I can't believe I'm doing this!" she squealed, bouncing up and down in the seat. "This is so cool!"

"Yeah, far out. Do you know where we're going, or am I driving around in circles?"

"It's just at the end of this street," Heather replied, leaning forward to peer out the windshield. "I'm pretty sure . . . yes! There!"

She pointed at a two-story house facing a quiet cul-de-sac. Its windows were black; the porch light was off. The bare trees in the front yard were barely discernible through the darkness. Nicole hoped the lack of lighting meant the occupants were home and already asleep, instead of out somewhere, ready to drive up and catch her in the act.

"What are you doing?" Heather demanded as Nicole cruised past their target. "Park the car!"

"I'm not going to park right in front of it, genius," Nicole retorted, growing more paranoid by the minute. She made a U-turn in the cul-de-sac and drove partway back down the street, finally stopping in the shadow of some pines.

"Okay," she said, taking a deep breath. "This is it. But I'm not getting out of this car until you tell me whose house that is."

Heather set her jaw stubbornly. Nicole could just make out her profile in the darkness.

"That wasn't part of the deal."

"Whose house is it, Heather?"

"How many beers did you have, Nicole?"

Nicole felt like strangling her, but she knew when she was beaten.

"Just swear to me that no one who goes to my school lives there. As long as this is between you and your little junior-high-school friends, I don't really care. But if it turns out I know anyone who lives here—"

"You don't," Heather said abruptly. "Now, come on."

They let themselves out of the Honda, being careful not to slam the doors, and began creeping up the street with their bags of toilet paper clutched to their chests. Ice crunched underfoot, and Nicole shivered from the mixture of cold and anxiety.

I must be crazy, she thought as she reached Heather's victim's front yard and took out her first roll of paper. *A person could get shot this way. Or the police could come any minute.*

"Whee!" Heather giggled, throwing a roll of paper in a big looping arc over a giant sycamore tree. Its streaming tail made it look like a comet, white against the night. Then the tail caught in the branches and the rest of the roll spiraled down to the ground. Scooping it up off the icy grass, Heather tossed it again, laughing as she did. It was obviously all a big game to her, but Nicole knew it wouldn't be funny if their parents found out.

"Will you shut up?" Nicole whispered furiously. "If we get caught, we're toast."

"You'd better make sure we *don't* get caught," Heather returned giddily. "Because if we do, I'm telling on you."

"I can't close up people's ears, you dweeb. Stop laughing."

Heather only smiled. "Paper faster."

Nicole fired the roll in her hand directly at Heather's head. Her sister dodged, and the toilet paper unwound across the yard, stopping in some bushes. Not bothering to retrieve the roll, Nicole whipped out another and tossed it blindly into the trees, just wanting to get out of there.

It took longer than Nicole had expected to use up all that paper. Each roll had to be tossed over and over again until it wound down to the cardboard core, and after the first two rolls Heather started checking to make sure Nicole wasn't cheating. Nicole TP'ed until her shoulder ached, all the while dreading a shout from within or the sudden glare of headlights from behind. Once a car came up to the intersection, sending her and Heather scurrying for cover, but it turned off at the corner, leaving Heather giggling happily and Nicole half sick from adrenaline.

At last only one roll remained. Paper draped the trees so thickly they looked like tissue tents, and every bush and shrub was veiled in white. Heather used the last roll to cover the ground, kicking it back and forth until it carpeted the grass.

"Finished!" she announced triumphantly, surveying her work with her hands on her hips. "Wow, this looks so cool!"

Nicole wasn't in the mood for sightseeing. "All right. We're done, so let's go."

"No. I have to leave my trademark."

"Your *what*? I'm not kidding, Heather. If you don't—"

"My trademark. So that Scott—uh, I mean, the person—will know it was me if I want him to later."

Heather took a playing card out of her jeans pocket and ripped it lengthwise into two pieces. Then, stealing up to the front door, she slipped one half under the mat.

"The Queen of Hearts!" she cried triumphantly, waving the other half in the air as she sprinted past Nicole toward the car. "And I have the matching piece!"

Nicole hesitated only as long as it took her to realize they were really leaving, then took off running after her sister. The two of them hurled their bodies into the car, Heather laughing like a maniac and Nicole shaking with relief. The engine spurted to life, and a minute later they were on their way home.

"We did it!" Heather shouted as they escaped down the silent street.

They had pulled it off. They were safe.

Thank God that's over, Nicole thought, completely drained by the experience. Heather could never tell on her now. If she went back on their deal, Nicole would simply reciprocate by ratting on her. Of course, then Nicole would be in trouble for TP'ing too.

She shook her head as she turned a corner and pointed the car toward home. *If Mom and Dad ever found out what I did at that party, TP'ing would look like a drop in the bucket.*

Eleven

"More tape," Jesse muttered, fumbling one-handed in the pocket of his letterman's jacket. His other hand held a long-stemmed red rose against the green metal door of Melanie's locker.

At that early hour of Thursday morning, there weren't many people in the hall. One or two walked by, peering at him curiously, but Jesse didn't care. Even if they recognized him, they didn't know whose locker he was decorating. For that matter, so what if they did? He had nothing to hide, and the whole school would know about him and Melanie soon enough.

Jesse put another, longer strip of tape over the rose stem, then two more spaced a couple of inches apart. This time when he let it go, the flower stayed in place, fixed at a jaunty angle across the door. He smiled, wondering what Melanie would think when she saw it.

She'll be surprised, he guessed. But surprised in a good way, he hoped.

It didn't take a psychiatrist to figure out that

Melanie was a little ambivalent about their relationship. Jesse caught the hints she dropped like bombs, and all her hands-off signals. But at the same time, he knew he was winning her over. Her lips might say she needed time, but her kisses said something else. They said she needed him.

And he was starting to think he needed her too. This wasn't about the challenge of dating her anymore, or how cute she looked in her cheerleading uniform. It wasn't about the fact that every guy at school knew who she was and wanted to know a lot more. Something was happening between them. Something real.

I think I'm falling in love.

All he knew for sure was that, more than ever before, he couldn't get Melanie Andrews out of his head. He didn't even want to anymore.

Taking a step back from her locker, he hesitated a minute, wondering if he should slip a note through the ventilation slots on its door. He'd have liked to ask her to the basketball game the next night but knew she had to cheer. He frowned, wishing cheerleading ended when football did. But maybe he could ask her to go off campus for lunch that day instead.

Jesse hesitated, then shook his head, deciding he'd rather ask her in person. He'd already memorized her new class schedule—it wouldn't be hard to find her.

His mind made up, he checked the tape on the rose one last time, then turned to walk away, nearly colliding with Lou Anne Simmons.

"Oh, hey, Lou Anne," he said, sidestepping around the cheerleader and continuing down the hall. The next second, he'd forgotten he'd ever seen her.

I wonder if Melanie's in the library, he thought hopefully, turning his steps in that direction.

"Did it come yet?" Jenna asked, bursting into the living room Thursday afternoon. Her mother was playing piano, practicing to lead the church choir on Sunday.

"It's in the kitchen," Mrs. Conrad replied without missing a beat.

"Thanks, Mom!"

Jenna dropped her backpack at the base of the stairs and ran into the kitchen, curiosity adding speed to her steps. Ever since her mother had told her about the Christian youth rally in Hollywood, Jenna had been on pins and needles for the brochure to come so she could find out who the band was.

The mail was stacked on the end of the counter adjacent to the breakfast nook. Jenna grabbed the whole pile and started riffling through it without even saying hello to Maggie and Allison, who were having a snack at the table. Maggie returned the favor by shooting her a venomous look and then continuing her conversation as though Jenna were invisible.

"*Anyway*," she said to Allison, "the entire eighth grade is trying to figure out who did it. It's all anyone is talking about."

"So, who did?" seventh-grader Allison asked breathlessly.

"Not me, that's all I know," Maggie said disgustedly. "I'd like to give whoever it was a big piece of my mind."

"Did what?" Jenna was afraid she'd be sorry she asked, but she couldn't resist the mystery.

"*Some*body toilet-papered Scott Jenner's house last night!" Maggie announced dramatically. "He brought Polaroids to school this morning, and it's the best job yet. By far."

Jenna was still digging through the bills and junk mail. "You mean they TP'ed his house before?"

"Not his. A bunch of others."

Jenna glanced up from the mail, confused. "Is it a contest?"

"Nooo." Maggie's voice made it clear how dense her sister was.

"So, what, then? And why are *you* so mad? Scott's the one who has to clean it up."

Maggie stared with wide eyes. "You don't even know what you're saying."

Allison nodded. "Not a clue, Jenna."

"Oh! Here it is!" Jenna cried, finally spotting the brochure. Forgetting her sisters completely, she hurried to open it. What had appeared to be a booklet turned out to be a colorful folded poster. She spread it on the counter, smoothing out the creases as she pored over the writing.

Friends! Fellowship! Fun! the top proclaimed in bold letters. *Join us at the 12th Annual Hearts for God Youth Conference, January 16–18.*

A collage of photos at odd angles showed teens participating in past events and apparently having a great time. Superimposed over the photos were columns of text describing the purpose of the conference and providing a detailed schedule of events.

"Concert, concert, concert," Jenna muttered impatiently, running her finger down the columns.

"It's them!" she screamed suddenly. "Fire & Water in concert!"

"Where?" Maggie demanded.

"In California." Jenna snatched up the poster and hugged it to her chest. "And I'm going to see them!"

"How?" Allison asked. "Mom and Dad aren't going to let you fly to California twice."

"No, silly. They're playing the weekend I'll be there with Leah."

"I thought you were going to a modeling contest," Maggie protested.

"I am. I'll do both."

"How? Are you going to duck out on Leah?"

"Of course not."

"Oh, I get it. Cloning, right?"

There was no denying that Maggie's skepticism was taking the edge off Jenna's excitement. What if she couldn't do both?

But then she had an idea. Her mom had a U.S. Girls itinerary somewhere, and Jenna was holding the complete schedule for the youth rally in her hands.

Spinning around abruptly, she ran to the living room.

A little planning, that's all that's needed here, she thought. *I still have plenty of time to make my very own schedule.*

And somehow, some way, I guarantee I'll wedge it all in.

Ben felt like a new man that Spirit Day Friday in his green-and-gold-striped rugby shirt. *Man. That's the key word*, he thought, strutting through the library with his head held high. At lunch that day, when the cheerleaders had run through the cafeteria yelling and waving their pom-poms, he'd almost burst with pride. *I kissed Angela Maldonado!* he'd wanted to shout.

Not that he ever would have. He was a gentleman, after all. But he *could* have—that was the main thing.

Later, he'd casually asked Melanie if she knew what Angela's new last class was. Sprinting directly to her door at the final bell, he'd made it through the crowd in the hallway just in time to see her and Tanya take off together, backpacks over their shoulders and pleated cheerleading skirts swinging at the tops of their thighs. He'd followed them at a distance until they'd gone into the library, but now that they'd taken seats and spread out their books, he was ready to make his move.

"Hi, Angela," he called, too loudly for the quiet zone. A few heads turned, but Ben didn't care. *Let them look!* he thought triumphantly. "How are you doing with your ma—*aaah!*"

Someone had left a chair partly blocking the aisle. Ben's foot caught one of its metal legs, and the next thing he knew he was hurtling forward, completely out of control. The edge of Angela's table loomed up to meet his face. He got his hands in front of him barely in time to avoid losing teeth, managing to push himself up into a mostly standing position. His feet were still so far out behind him, though, he looked ready for a wheelbarrow race.

"Uh, hi, Angela," he said, his face only inches from hers.

For the first time since he had met her, she seemed embarrassed by his clumsiness. Her cheeks turned a little pinker, and she didn't meet his eyes. "Hi, Ben."

"Thanks for dropping in," Tanya added with a chuckle. "Can we help you?"

There were snickers at the neighboring tables. Ben scrambled to his feet and attempted to muster some dignity. "Actually, I was wondering if I could help you. Do you have any more of those math problems?"

"No," Angela said quickly. "I mean, uh, thanks, but I've got it now." She looked down at her book.

Tanya gave him one last glance, then returned to her book too.

Ben struck a casual pose, leaning against the front edge of their table. "So, I really helped you then, huh?"

Angela looked back up. "Yeah. I already said you did."

Oh, you did a lot more than that, Ben thought, trying to convey that idea with a wink.

"Is there something in your eye?"

"My, uh, contact," Ben said, panicking. "Sometimes they still bother me."

"Maybe you ought to go back to glasses."

"No, no. See? All better." He stared her down with both eyes open. Wide open.

"What?" she asked him defensively, shaking her head and turning her palms right side up. "Do you want something, Ben?"

"Me? No."

"Then . . . ?"

Why are you looking at me like that? was what he knew she meant. He couldn't even have said. He supposed he just wanted to see something, some little sign, that Angela acknowledged what had happened between them.

I don't expect her to come right out and say 'Hey, great kissing you' or anything, but she could give me a little nod. A wink. Anything.

It was becoming pretty clear that wasn't going to happen, though. In fact, Angela already seemed to have forgotten the entire incident. Hadn't it been as great for her as it was for him?

A sudden panic gripped him—had he done something horribly wrong?

"We're kind of busy, Ben," said Tanya. "We're *supposed* to be, anyway."

"Huh? Oh. Right." He could feel himself blushing. "I was, um, going anyway. I have some reading to do."

Did he ever! As soon as he could find a private corner, he was going to reread the entire kissing handbook.

"I *guess* this is the place," Leah said to herself, hesitating uncertainly outside a sprawling office building Friday evening.

She and Miguel had made up after their fight, but things still weren't back to normal between them. At lunchtime the last three days, getting him to talk about his new job had been like pulling teeth, while she avoided all mention of the U.S. Girls contest and college. That left them with the weather, their new classes, and a lot of other chitchat that might have been interesting—if they both hadn't been so aware of all the real subjects they were avoiding.

Nervous and not sure she should be there, Leah glanced up and down the deserted sidewalk in front of the building, then took a tentative step forward. The light was nearly gone outside, and she could see through the entry glass that the interior lobby was darkened too. Only a few little security lights allowed her to make out the massive wood reception desk and the clusters of darkly upholstered chairs.

"I didn't expect it to look like this," she muttered. She'd wanted to surprise Miguel when he got off work, so she hadn't come right out and asked for the address of his job site, but from the few things he'd said she'd been sure she could find the right building. Now she wasn't sure at all.

Walking slowly to the front door, she gave it a gentle push, fully expecting it to be locked. To her surprise, it swung open easily, admitting her into the lobby. And then the sharp scent of paint let her know she was in the right place.

"Miguel?" she called softly, following her nose.

On the left side of the lobby, an interior door was propped open. Leah walked that way and discovered a long hall on the other side. The odor of paint in the hall was even stronger, and down near the end light spilled through a side door, illuminating a patch of patterned carpet. Slipping into the hallway, Leah strode toward the light, confident that she'd found Miguel.

Sure enough, his voice carried to her just before she reached the doorway.

"It feels so good to be *doing* something again," he was saying, his tone more cheerful than Leah had heard it for days. "School is nothing but talking, talking, talking, you know? Lately it seems like talking is all I do."

A perfect female giggle floated to Leah's ears, freezing her in the hallway. "I can't tell you how glad I am to have graduated. It feels like getting out of jail."

"Well, just one more semester, then I'm free too."

Free? Leah's eyebrows shot up. *And who's he talking to?*

She took the last few steps to the open door and stood looking into a large conference room. Dropcloths draped a mound of furniture near the center and protected the carpeted floor. The windows were partly hidden, masked with tape and thin plastic.

Miguel stood with his back to the door, his old jeans and T-shirt speckled with white. The paper cap he wore was spattered as well, and so was the skin of his forearms. But paint wasn't the only thing clinging to Miguel's arm—a gorgeous brunette dressed in old painting clothes rested her hand there as if she owned him. Leah faced her from the doorway, stunned into silence. The girl's sharply arched brows were as dark as her hair, her eyes were amethyst, and the smile under her high cheekbones was whiter than any new paint.

Leah realized in that moment that she had never truly been jealous before. She was completely unprepared for the racing heart and roaring in her ears that accompanied the sight of that girl's hand on her boyfriend's arm. She was so upset she could barely breathe.

The beauty finally noticed her. "One second," she told Miguel with a flirtatious twitch of her perfect nose. Looking over his shoulder, she met Leah's gaze. "Can I help you?"

"I—I—"

"Leah!" Miguel exclaimed happily, turning around to face her. The offending hand slid off his arm like water. "What are you doing here?"

"I thought maybe I could take you to dinner," she said, her gaze still stuck on those violet eyes. "That is, if you're done here."

"Sure. We're done." He turned back to the brunette. "So what time tomorrow? Eight o'clock?"

"Bright and early." The girl smiled again, showing dimples as well as cheekbones. "Aren't you going to introduce me to your friend?"

"Oh, yeah. Sabrina, this is my girlfriend, Leah. Leah, Sabrina Ambrosi."

"Nice to meet you," Leah said through gritted teeth.

135

"Same here. Okay, Miguel, I'll see you tomorrow." Sabrina turned and sauntered off toward the back of the room, where some painting supplies were still strewn about.

Leah watched her go, acutely aware of the way the girl's faded jeans hugged curves Leah didn't have. She didn't even want to imagine what additional curves might be lurking beneath Sabrina's loose shirt.

Miguel tugged at her hand. "So are we going, or what?"

"Huh? Yeah. Let's take my dad's car to Burger City, and afterwards we'll swing back by here for yours." It would have been easier to drive separate cars to the restaurant, but Leah didn't want to let him out of her sight until she knew what was going on.

Once she had him in her car, though, she couldn't decide what to say. She kept waiting for him to voluntarily illuminate her on the subject of Sabrina Ambrosi—and her very good reason for touching any part of his body—but Miguel only talked of the weather, as they'd been doing for three days.

"So what about this snowstorm?" he asked, looking upward through his window, as if anyone could really see clouds through that blackness. "I heard it was coming tonight for sure."

"I heard only flurries. Miguel, who's Sabrina?"

"What do you mean?" he asked, puzzled. "I just introduced you to her."

"I mean, who *is* she?" Leah snapped.

"Well, she's the boss's daughter. Or actually, the boss, I guess. She's running the crew on my painting job."

"She's in *charge*? How old is she?"

"Eighteen. Why?"

"I just . . . I don't know. Why was her hand on your arm?"

"When?" He looked positively mystified.

"When I came to the door! She had her hand on your arm like this." Keeping one hand on the wheel, Leah reached across the gearshift to demonstrate with the other, although Sabrina's finger pressure had likely been nothing compared to hers.

Miguel shrugged. "If she did, I didn't notice. Sabrina and I have known each other forever."

"Forever," Leah repeated flatly, but she was getting more freaked out by the minute.

"Well . . . yeah. Our dads were friends. And she went to Sacred Heart, same as Rosa. She's been hanging around her father's construction sites since she was old enough to wear a hard hat, so I see her every summer, and usually once or twice in between."

Leah suddenly remembered the conversation she had overheard from the hallway. "If she graduated in June, why isn't she at college?"

"What for?" Miguel asked, his irritation obvious at the mention of the C word. "She's learning everything she needs to know right here."

Leah could think of a million reasons—if she'd dared to go down that road.

"And the other guys do what she says?" she asked instead. "They don't give her a hard time on the job?"

Miguel looked at her as if she'd gone crazy. "Not if they want to live. Her father's the boss, remember? Besides, uh . . ." He hesitated, pulling at a frayed thread on his jeans. "Did you happen to get a good look at her?"

Unfortunately, Leah thought, feeling her heart sink down to her stomach. He even *admitted* she was gorgeous.

And that was one admission she could do without.

Twelve

"**D**o you have to walk so close?" Melanie asked Jesse irritably. "How about giving me a little room?"

Jesse only smirked as the two of them crossed the snow-dusted parking lot at Clearwater Crossing Park. "I know, I know. You need your space."

His teasing tone made it clear he didn't know at all. He seemed to have absolutely no idea how mad at him she was. If there hadn't been snow on the ground, she'd have pedaled her bike to the park just to avoid riding with him.

He must have lost his mind to have taped that rose to my locker, she thought, still fuming. He should have known that *someone* was going to see him. But the fact that the someone who did was Lou Anne Simmons, Vanessa's right-hand brownnoser, should have triggered a four-bell alarm. *He could at least have warned me.*

Melanie opened her mouth to tell him off for the hours of petty backbiting Vanessa had subjected her to at the basketball game Friday night; then she abruptly shut it again. The way she was feeling just then, she didn't even trust herself to speak to him.

"Hey, you guys! Hurry up!" Jenna called from the edge of the parking lot. The Junior Explorers' bus was parked behind the activities center, its nose pointed out toward the pavement, and Jenna and the rest of Eight Prime were gathered in a tight little knot at its side. "Come see what they did to the bus!"

Melanie began to trot, glad of the excuse to put some distance between her and Jesse, but Mr. Clueless stayed right on her heels, crowding her until they reached the others and got their first good look at the new paint job.

"Didn't it come out great?" Peter asked. "They really did a good job."

Melanie nodded silently, an unexpected lump in her throat. *Remembering Kurt Englbehrt*—that's what the blue letters said. And suddenly remembering was exactly what she was doing. Glancing around at her friend's solemn faces, she had a feeling she wasn't the only one.

"I think it came out perfect," said Nicole, not even adding that pink would have looked better.

Miguel stretched out a hand to touch the *K* in Kurt's name, brushing his gloved fingers down the cold metal siding. Leah held tight to his other hand and let her free fingers touch the *E*.

"Wow. It's just . . . I don't know," said Ben, fumbling for the words. "This just makes it all seem so much more . . . real."

"It does," said Jenna. "I know what you mean."

Peter closed his eyes, and Melanie knew he was praying for Kurt, just as he'd promised he would. Even though Kurt's life had ended, Peter's prayers went on. Melanie wondered what he prayed for now, but she didn't wonder why. That part she understood.

"Well, I wish I had more time, but I have to go back in and help Chris with the Junior Explorers," Peter said when he opened his eyes. He gestured behind him at the activities center. "You're all welcome to come hang out. Or if not . . ."

"I will," Melanie said. "I want to see Amy."

"Me too," Jesse said immediately. "I want to see Amy too."

Melanie winced. Could he possibly be more blatant? No one else seemed to notice, however, as one by one the others opted to come along.

"Is Elton here today?" Ben asked. "He likes me. I think."

Peter laughed and punched Ben's shoulders. "You don't sound too sure. Don't you know?"

"I never know," Ben replied cryptically, pulling his parka hood down over his face as he set off toward the building.

Inside the activities center, the kids were literally bouncing off the walls. Chris had set up two long strips of tumbling mats with matching strips propped up against the adjacent walls. The girls were mostly rolling or cartwheeling down the mats on the floor, while the boys delivered fancy karate kicks to the uprights. Priscilla was the one exception to the rule, putting the boys to shame with the sheer fury and inventiveness of her footwork.

"Melanie!" Amy shouted, spotting her just inside the doorway. "Melanie, hi!"

She barreled across the room, barely giving Melanie time to brace herself before wrapping a fierce hug around her legs.

"Hi, you," Melanie said fondly, leaning down to hug Amy back. "What are you playing?"

"Olympics." Amy grabbed her by the hand and started pulling her toward the mats. "Except that Lisa is hogging all the metals."

She pointed accusingly at the curly-topped blonde, who stood off to one side of the action with four or five bright plastic leis around her neck.

"You mean medals," Jesse corrected, following them like an eager little puppy.

A too-eager little puppy, Melanie thought. *Doesn't he have any self-respect?* Then another thought scared her to death. *Is this what he's going to be like from now on?*

She stopped walking so abruptly that Jesse bumped into her back. "Why don't you go play with Jason?" she suggested, pointing.

Jason and Danny still hadn't noticed Eight Prime's arrival in their determination to beat the wall to a pulp.

"Well, okay. But I'd rather be with you." He hovered at her side, his hand brushing hers in an obvious way before he set off across the large room.

"Brother," Melanie muttered under her breath.

"Why is Jesse acting so weird?" Amy asked.

"I have no idea." Just because they had some sort of minor little thing going on didn't mean he had to let it show for the whole world. Not only that, but there was such a thing as too much attention. His behavior was past uncool—it was ridiculous. He wasn't even acting like the guy she'd thought she was getting involved with anymore. She'd be mortified if anyone in Eight Prime noticed the way he was carrying on.

This is a nightmare, she thought as she and Amy went to join the little girls. *He'd better shape up soon or he's gone.*

"Oh! And I *have* to do *this*," Jenna mumbled, circling another event on her Hearts for God conference poster. She was stretched out on her stomach on her bed, papers scattered everywhere and a clipboard under the poster to give her a hard writing surface. Reaching for the U.S. Girls itinerary, she began checking to see if that event time looked clear or if there was yet another conflict.

The truth of the matter was that planning wasn't getting her nearly as far as she'd hoped. There were a million things she wanted to do at the youth rally, but both it and the modeling contest had jam-packed calendars. How could she juggle events when there weren't any gaps in the schedule? The worst news of all was that the final contest and the concert were on the same night—the last night. The only ray of hope was that the contest started a little earlier. If Fire & Water had a warm-up band . . .

Jenna's door opened and Caitlin walked in, her fair cheeks flushed.

"Mail came," she said, staring down at the single white envelope she carried.

"Is it for me?"

"No." Caitlin dropped into a sitting position on her bed, still staring. "It's for me," she said finally, holding the envelope up to Jenna's view. "From David Altmann."

"No way!" Jenna screamed, leaping to her feet. "Oh, Caitlin! Open it right now!" She jumped up and down between their twin beds, beside herself with excitement.

"What do you think he wants?" Caitlin asked, not moving.

"What do you mean, what does he want? If he's writing you a letter, he must like you. Come on, Cat, open it. The suspense is killing me."

A smile crept onto Caitlin's face as she flipped the letter over. Slowly—*so* slowly—she ran her thumb beneath the flap to break the seal and drew out a single sheet of notebook paper. Jenna nearly groaned at the discovery that there wasn't any writing on the back for her to peek at.

"What, what, what?" she urged impatiently. "What does he say?"

Caitlin began reading, her eyes flying down the words. Then, suddenly, the smile left her lips and the color drained from her cheeks. She put the letter down abruptly, covering it with both hands.

"Caitlin, what's the matter? Let me see it." Jenna reached to grab the letter, but Caitlin snatched it back, crumpling it into a tight little ball.

"It's nothing," she said, her voice barely a whisper. "It's not even really a letter. He just wants . . . he wants Mary Beth's college address so that he can write to her."

"He *what?*" Jenna's voice rose to an indignant screech. "You mean she *stole* him from you? I can't believe it!"

"Then don't, because it isn't true."

Caitlin's chin had dropped; her shoulders slumped. Jenna imagined she saw her sister withering before her eyes. All the progress Caitlin had made in coming out of her shell had been wiped away by a few simple words.

"No, it's Mary Beth's fault. She was flirting with him! She didn't have to be so funny and nice. She's not funny and nice to *us*."

"Please, Jenna, I—"

"How dare she try to take him away from—"

"She didn't *take* him," Caitlin insisted, with a hint of her more recent strength. "He isn't mine."

"But he could have been! I'm going to call Peter right now and—"

"No, you're not!" Caitlin said quickly. "That's the last thing you're going to do."

"But why?" Jenna wailed. "Peter and I could get this all straightened out in an hour. I'll bet David doesn't even know that you—"

"And he isn't going to. Think about it, Jenna. If you liked a guy and he didn't like you back, would you want him to know all about it?"

The words had more impact than Caitlin had probably intended. Jenna's cheeks flushed scarlet as she remembered her futile crush on Miguel del Rios. The way things had worked out with Peter had enabled her to put that disaster out of her mind, but for one instant all the pain and disappointment came flooding back, and she knew she would die of embarrassment if Miguel ever found out. Defeated, she dropped onto the bed beside Caitlin and put an arm around her shoulders.

"I'm so sorry, Cat," she said from the bottom of her aching heart. "If there's anything I can do . . ."

Caitlin shook her head. The motion knocked loose the tears that had pooled in her brown eyes. They ran down her cheeks unchecked as she squeezed the crumpled letter into an even smaller ball. "It just hurts so much," she whimpered. "You have no idea."

Jenna hugged her sister tighter, wishing that were true.

"Will you look at that?" Mrs. Brewster demanded, pointing ahead through the windshield. Nicole and her family were on their way home from Sunday services, her father at the wheel. "This entire thing is getting out of hand."

From the backseat of the Honda, Nicole and Heather strained forward to see what their mother was talking about, then abruptly sat back again, their expressions as blank as they could make them. Someone had TP'ed a house a couple of blocks from their own.

Compared to the job the Brewster girls had done, the house the Honda was passing was strictly an amateur effort—ten rolls at the most. The little bit of snow still clinging to the ground added to the overall whiteness, making the papering look more impressive than it actually was.

"I don't know what's wrong with kids today," Mrs. Brewster complained to her husband. "Not to mention their parents! I was raised to believe that people were supposed to *control* their children."

She'd have had a heart attack if she'd seen the house

Heather and I did, Nicole thought, sinking a little lower in her seat.

"Well, you know how it is now," Mr. Brewster said. "What with day care and all these latchkey kids, their parents don't even know what they're doing ninety percent of the time."

"True. Thank heavens I've managed to stay home and raise our children right." Mrs. Brewster turned to flash the occupants of the backseat a naive smile that struck ice into Nicole's heart. If her mom ever found out . . .

"And, of course, we were blessed with particularly good children to begin with," Mr. Brewster boasted, adding his smile to hers.

Or her dad, for that matter . . .

Nicole glanced sideways to see if her sister shared her panic. But instead of exhibiting the belated dread that was gripping Nicole, Heather was glowing with pride.

Surely she doesn't believe all that stuff Mom and Dad just said! Even Heather wasn't that dumb. *So, what, then? What's she so happy about?*

The answer came in a flash. *She's glad we didn't get caught.*

Nicole took a deep breath, sharing her sister's relief.

Maybe Heather was smarter than she'd thought.

Thirteen

Okay. Here she comes, Ben thought, psyching himself up.

Angela was walking down the main hallway between morning classes, looking even more beautiful than usual. She was wearing a new outfit that Monday—a winter-white sweater and slacks. They looked so soft and cuddly that Ben found his right hand floating up to touch them.

Just be cool, he thought, forcing his hand down in a hurry. *And whatever you do—don't blow it again this time!*

He pulled himself up taller, then changed his mind and leaned against the locker next to hers. He had everything planned out. In fact, he'd been planning it all weekend.

There was no denying that Angela hadn't reacted to him too well on Friday, but he thought he'd figured out why: The problem hadn't been his kissing, it had been his clumsiness. How could he have expected any sort of secret signal after the scene he'd created in front of the entire library?

This time I'll be smooth, he promised himself, watching Angela take the last few steps to her locker. *This time I won't give her any excuse*.

"Hi, Angela!" he said when she was beside him. He had pitched his voice at the perfect level—loud enough for her to hear it over the other noises in the hallway, not loud enough to attract attention.

"Hi, Ben," she returned cheerfully, spinning her combination lock. "What are you doing here?"

"Waiting for you."

"Oh?" Her smile lost a little wattage. "Why?"

"Well . . . I just thought I'd say hello. *You* know."

The confusion in her eyes made it clear she didn't know at all. "You're just hanging around here in the hall, instead of going to class, because you wanted to say hi to me?"

The way she said it made him sound kind of desperate.

"Is there something wrong with wanting to say hi?"

He winced as soon as the words left his mouth. The way he'd said *that* made him sound *really* desperate.

"Uh, no. I guess not." Angela swung her locker door open and started digging through the books inside. "I don't have a lot of time, though."

"I know. You have to get to algebra, right?"

She stopped rummaging and looked at him hard. "Do you know my whole schedule or something?"

"No," Ben lied quickly, sensing "No" was the right answer.

She shuddered a little, then smiled, relieved. "Good, because that would have been kind of creepy."

Creepy? he thought. *Why creepy?*

Because she doesn't like you, genius! he answered himself immediately. *She doesn't want you following her all over school like some pathetic little mascot.*

No, she does too like me, he argued. *She's always been nice, and she laughs at my jokes, and she danced with me at homecoming. Besides, if she doesn't like me, then why did she kiss me?*

She didn't kiss you on purpose. You practically had to beg her first. And then, when she leaned in for that pity peck, you're the one who twisted around and made it lip to lip. You're lucky she's even still talking to you.

A flush crept up his cheeks at the realization. Not only had he taken advantage of a nice person, he'd been dumb enough to hope she'd liked it.

"Well, you'd better get to class," he said abruptly, spinning around and starting to dash off.

"Wait, Ben."

He stopped, his back still toward her.

"Is everything okay?"

He nodded.

"You and I . . . I mean, you weren't thinking . . . We're just kind of friends, right?"

"Right." He glanced back over his shoulder, trying to smile as if he hadn't expected anything else. Then he took off down the hallway as fast as he could go without running.

Just kind of friends, he repeated as he pushed through the crowd. *That's even worse than just friends. That's like . . . like nothing!*

Detouring down a side hall, Ben stopped against the wall and ripped his backpack open, pulling at the zipper tabs so roughly he broke the cord on one. Snatching out the paper-covered kissing handbook, he spiked it into a nearby trash can, where it sank until it was covered by papers and other garbage. He only wished he could tear it to shreds, or burn it on the front steps of the school, or something a lot more in keeping with his opinion of its useless advice.

Stupid book! Sure, it covered techniques he'd never dreamed of—and in step-by-step detail. But in its obsession with "how," not a single word had ever been devoted to "why." *Nowhere in that whole stupid book does it mention that two people who are kissing ought to actually like each other!*

Ben gave the trash can one last shove, then hurried off to class, feeling like the biggest fool in the world. Being kissed by someone who didn't mean it was worse than never having been kissed at all.

Leah sat up in bed. "I'm never going to get any sleep," she muttered, flipping on the light on her nightstand. "I might as well do something useful."

Plumping up her pillows, she grabbed an assigned novel from its place next to the lamp. She'd read more than half the book the night before—she hadn't been able to sleep then, either—and she opened to the place she had left her marker. *Might as well finish it off*, she thought. Although, as poorly as she was concentrating, she was probably going to have to read the entire thing again.

She smoothed the right page flat and stared at it blankly.

Why did he have to take that stupid job? The question had been running through her head night and day since she'd first learned about Miguel's unexpected employment, but now that she'd met Sabrina Ambrosi, it had assumed a new kind of urgency. *Is he trying to teach me a lesson?*

The book dropped to her lap. *For what? No, this isn't about me. He just wants to make some money so his family can get a new place.*

At least she hoped that was all that was going on. Because the conversation she'd overheard him having with Sabrina wouldn't leave her mind either.

What did he mean, that he'd be free after this semester? He made it sound like he wants me to leave.

She shook her head impatiently. She knew that wasn't true.

I hope Sabrina knows it too.

Every time Leah remembered the possessive way that girl had been touching his arm, it made her wish Miguel's work experience was in any other field. The truth was, she was more than jealous now, she was scared. Miguel had worked three afternoons the previous week, all day Saturday, and late that Monday as well. Leah had barely even seen him.

But Sabrina was seeing him plenty. At lunch in the cafeteria it was Sabrina this and Sabrina that, as if he were completely unaware that Leah might not be his female boss's biggest fan. The worst part was that he and Sabrina had so much in common. Sabrina was going to be a contractor, like her father, and Miguel had once planned to be a contractor too. Sabrina was Catholic; Miguel was Catholic. Sabrina was gorgeous; Miguel was gorgeous. Sabrina was probably going to stay in Clearwater Crossing her whole life, and Miguel . . .

"Oh, this is crazy!" Leah exclaimed, forgetting that her parents were asleep and throwing her book off the bed. "I've got to stop thinking like this."

She lay back against the pillows and closed her eyes, looking for another subject to distract her.

But all she came up with was the U.S. Girls contest, and the fact that she was going to be out of town for a whole three-day weekend, plus half of two more days for traveling. And was she paranoid, or was Miss Junior Contractor just dying for that to happen? Leah was pretty sure her boyfriend could resist his supervisor's more than obvious charms for the duration of the modeling contest, but what about in September? If Leah decided to go off to college, and if

Miguel decided to stay at home with Sabrina the teenage witch . . .

"Stop it!" she exclaimed, snapping her eyes wide open again. "It's only January. If you keep worrying this way, you'll go crazy before fall."

Too late. She was already going crazy.

And she hated the fact that she was so scared.

After all, she loved Miguel. She trusted Miguel. If their relationship was going to last a lifetime, it ought to survive the next few months.

A *lifetime?* The idea brought her right out of bed. She wandered over to the book she'd thrown, picked it up, and set it on her desk without seeing it. She'd never really thought in terms of forever. Or at least she'd never admitted it.

But I don't want to lose him. I can't.

I'm not going to.

Whatever it took, she'd figure out a way to stay together. If he was so set on working, couldn't he move to wherever she decided to go to school and get a job there? Why did she have to stay in Clearwater Crossing? No, there were a million different possibilities, and she owed it to them both to think of every single one.

Grabbing a pencil and pad off her desk, she climbed back into bed.

"This is a test, like any other," she said.

Then, in her best teacher's voice, "Please number your papers from one to fifty."

Leah began numbering eagerly. If there were fifty

ways to leave a lover, like the old song said, there had to be fifty ways to stay with one too.

"You don't even know whose house it was?" Courtney chortled.

To take her friend's mind off Jeff, Nicole had chosen that Tuesday to finally confess the big TP caper.

"Some friend of Heather's—I don't know. But she swore no one who went to this school lived there."

Nicole glanced nervously around the packed cafeteria, half afraid of being overheard and challenged on that point. The two girls had the wall end of a table to themselves, though, and privacy was nearly assured under the covering noise from the rest of the lunch crowd. "I can't believe she even wanted to do it, actually. She's such a goody-goody."

"*I* can't believe she talked *you* into it. Since when did you start doing favors for Heather?"

"Well, it was just kind of a . . . a mutual thing, and—"

"She has something on you!" Courtney said, a spark of wonder in her green eyes. "Heather, a blackmailer! I'm impressed."

"Yeah, well, I'm sure she could still learn a few tricks from you."

Courtney smiled and helped herself to the dessert on Nicole's tray. "Who couldn't? So what did you do? I'm dying to hear this."

"Nothing. I broke a stupid vase, is all. But Heather found out I was drinking at the New Year's party, and she was going to tell Mom I was drunk, which is a total lie."

Courtney laughed. "You weren't exactly sober."

"No, but I wasn't actually . . . it was just easier to give the little creep what she wanted."

"Sure. That's why you did it." Courtney nodded sagely. "Why didn't you tell me about this before?"

"I don't know. I guess I was just saving it for a day like today, when you really needed a lift."

"Yeah. Or until you were sure you had gotten away with it."

Nicole blinked. She had nearly forgotten how it had been in the days before Jeff and Eight Prime had come along. Back then, Courtney had known her better than she'd known herself.

"I missed you, do you know that?" Nicole said. "I think I just realized how much."

Courtney grinned at the compliment. "Then Jeff's loss is your gain. Yours and some lucky new guy's."

"I thought you said we weren't going to date for a while!"

"What do you want? It's been a whole week." Courtney's eyes held all their old familiar mischief.

Nicole heaved a mock sigh. "Do you have some *particular* lucky guy in mind?"

"I'll know him when I see him," Courtney said mysteriously.

"Well, just don't pick out any more dates for me."

"Yeah, yeah. So what are we doing this weekend?"

"This weekend?" Nicole repeated nervously.

"Saturday, Sunday, and Monday. You know?" Courtney's tone was suspicious. "What's up?"

Nicole had prepared and prepared for the discussion they were about to have. And even though she was nervous, she was also positive she was right. Courtney was just going to have to compromise, for once.

"Well . . . it's just that I'm leaving on Friday for the U.S. Girls contest. Remember?"

Nicole had thought adding the word *remember* was a nice touch, as though Courtney had known about her departure all along. Courtney, however, seemed unimpressed by her finesse.

"What?" she screeched, making heads turn in the cafeteria. "You told me you weren't going to that!"

"No, Court," Nicole corrected swiftly. "*You* told *me*. I never said I wouldn't."

"You—You let me think so," Courtney sputtered angrily.

"Look, Courtney," Nicole pleaded. "I don't think you're being very fair. I'm sorry Leah didn't invite you, but can't you just let it go? I was there for you when you needed a friend. Now can't you be happy for me?"

"That's not the same thing. I didn't have any choice about breaking up with Jeff." Courtney's voice caught a little at the mention of her ex's name. "You can't compare something like that to taking a vacation. You want to be there for me? Be there for me this weekend."

"You're not being reasonable, Court—"

"I don't have to be reasonable! If you were really my friend, you wouldn't *want* to go on that trip."

"If you were really *my* friend, you wouldn't want me to stay home. You know how I feel about modeling. Besides, Leah only won that trip because of me."

"So what you're saying is that your ridiculous obsession with modeling is more important than our friendship." Courtney had finally lowered her voice. Now it rasped like sandpaper.

"I never said that," Nicole replied, angered by Courtney's choice of words. "But it sounds like you just did."

"I can tell you this, Nicole: If you go on that trip, don't think we're still best friends."

"What's that supposed to mean?"

Courtney stood up and hoisted her backpack onto her shoulder. "It means that all my *other* friends still have plenty of time for me."

"Then why don't you let one of them entertain you this weekend?"

"Go to L.A. and they'll be entertaining me a lot longer," Courtney threatened. Then, turning abruptly, she stormed out of the cafeteria, her red hair streaming behind her.

"Great," Nicole groaned as she watched her friend stalk off. "Way to compromise, Court."

Fourteen

Ben and Mark were fooling around in the CCHS computer lab after school on Wednesday, checking out one of Ben's dad's new programs, when a girl Ben only vaguely recognized walked in, scanned the room, and happened to notice them. Her expression changed in an instant, from slightly lost and confused to completely furious.

"Uh-oh," Mark whispered as she bypassed the computer signup sheet and walked toward them. He ducked his head behind the monitor he and Ben were using, obviously trying to hide, but his maneuvering was in vain.

"It's you, isn't it?" the girl accused him, completely ignoring Ben and the numerous QUIET, PLEASE signs plastered all over the lab. "You're the little worm going around saying he kissed me at the New Year's party!"

And suddenly Ben remembered where he'd seen her before. She was the girl from Mark's chemistry class. The one he *had* been saying he kissed.

"No way, Candice!" Mark said quickly. "Why would I do a thing like that?"

"I can think of a hundred reasons. *You* sure don't have anything to lose, do you?"

A student lab monitor hustled over to their table from the counter at the front of the room. "Keep it down or you're all out of here," he warned. "People are trying to work."

"We were leaving anyway." Mark stood up and grabbed his pack off the back of the chair.

His friend was halfway to the door before Ben realized he was being left behind. Hurriedly ejecting his father's CD from the computer, he scrambled to catch up.

"I'd better not hear any more rumors with my name in them!" Candice yelled at their backs.

Mark only walked faster, making Ben almost jog.

"Hey, slow down," Ben panted.

But it wasn't until he reached a vacant stairwell at the end of the hall that Mark finally let Ben close the distance between them.

The two of them faced off silently until Mark shrugged and dropped his gaze. "So, I guess you think I'm a total loser now."

"No." Ben hadn't had time to think. "I just don't understand."

"What's to understand?"

"I don't know."

Mark glowered. His entire demeanor had changed, from friendly and happy to sullen and secretive.

Ben shuffled his feet uncomfortably, feeling totally out of his depth. "I guess I'd better . . . You know what? I'm just going to go." He turned to leave.

But Mark stopped him in midstep. "No, don't," he said abruptly. "Look, I obviously never kissed Candice. What do you expect me to say?"

Ben turned slowly back around. "Well, you could tell me why you lied about it."

Mark looked off, as if to avoid answering, but when his eyes came back they were oddly defiant. "It's just . . . I've never kissed anyone, all right?"

"*What?* Then why—"

"Because I was tired of being the only one! Can you understand *that?* The thing is, I only told you and a couple of other people I was sure would never tell Candice. I don't know how it got back to her."

Mark dropped his backpack to the floor, then sat down beside it, burying his face in his arms. "I feel like a total idiot."

Ben hesitated a long, awkward moment, then joined his friend on the floor. "Don't." Raising a hand to pat Mark's shoulder, he chickened out and scratched his own head instead. "I mean, I wish you hadn't lied to me, but I know why you did."

Mark looked up. "Why?"

"Because it's embarrassing, never having kissed

anyone. It makes you feel like you're . . . I don't know. Slow or something."

"How would you know? I mean, you've kissed people. Right?"

For a moment Ben considered claiming Angela. As far as bragging rights went, Candice Barns couldn't hold a candle to her. Besides, saying he'd kissed Angela wouldn't be a lie—exactly—and it would serve Mark right for causing him so much stress. But if he told that story, how could he be sure it wouldn't get around the same way Mark's lie had? The last thing he wanted was to embarrass Angela any more than he already had.

"No," he said at last. "Not really. Not so it mattered, anyway."

Mark's eyes narrowed a little, as if he suspected Ben of humoring him, but then he nodded, relieved.

"So what about that nineteen-year-old you told me about?" Ben asked. "Was that all made up too?"

More color stained Mark's cheeks. "Linda? Total fantasy. Except that she is a friend of my sister's. And she is just as hot as I said. Maybe this summer . . ."

"When she's twenty? Dream on."

Ben stood up and offered Mark a hand. Mark accepted and let Ben jerk him to his feet.

"So, do you want to go back to the computer lab?" Ben asked. "You barely saw any of my dad's new program."

"Back in there with Candice? You're kidding, right?"

"Yeah," Ben admitted. "Maybe you'd better give Candice a year or two to cool off."

Mark grinned sheepishly. "You think it's going to take that long? I was planning on asking her to the prom."

"You know, that's a good idea. Do it in a big crowd, and I'll be there with a video camera."

"Yeah, yeah. Call the yearbook committee. Listen, why don't we go over to your house?" Mark suggested. "Your computer must put that junk in the lab to shame."

"Well, it's just that . . ." *I never invite anyone over,* Ben finished silently, thinking of his mother. She'd be sure to hover over them the entire time and ask a million embarrassing questions. Not to mention the shock of first seeing her in a housedress.

On the other hand, he and Mark had bigger secrets between them now than an overweight mother. And if they were really going to be friends, there had to be a certain amount of trust. "Okay, sure. Why not?"

"Cool," Mark said as they headed for the door. "Maybe this weekend you can come over and hang at my house."

"Yeah. Maybe."

But as they walked out to the bus stop, Ben turned his thoughts to more important issues. The romantic failures he and Mark had so recently suffered had made one thing suddenly clear.

I'm going to make a new resolution, he decided. *The next time I kiss somebody—even someone as hot as Angela—it's going to mean something. It's not going to be sneaky, and it's not going to be an accident. It's going to be the kind of thing I can shout to the whole wide world.*

The next time I kiss somebody, I'm going to be in love.

"Stop, stop, stop!" shouted Sandra Kincaid, CCHS's cheerleading coach. The music echoing through the gym suddenly went silent. "That's the sloppiest pattern I ever saw."

Vanessa glared at Melanie. "You can't expect the tall people to hit their positions if the short people don't get out of their way."

She had been saying things like that all practice, and Melanie had had enough. "Oh, that's a total crock of—"

"Stop it right now, both of you," Sandra snapped. She pointed at Vanessa with one red-tipped finger. "You may be the captain, but I'm in charge. I'll decide what the problems are. Right now the problem seems to be that you and Tiffany aren't moving fast enough."

"Me!" Tiffany Barrett protested. "Don't drag me into their catfight. I swear I never dated the guy."

Sandra's brown eyes narrowed, but a titter from Cindy egged Tiffany on. "I mean, for one thing, he's only a *junior*," she said, baiting their senior squad leader.

"For another, he has better taste," Vanessa snarled back.

"Obviously not," said Melanie, locking eyes with Vanessa.

"All right, that's it," Sandra declared. "If you all want to look like a grade-school squad at the basketball game next week, don't let me stop you. I'm not going to waste my time coaching you when you obviously have much smaller things on your minds. Go on. Hit the locker room."

Their coach bent over to pick up her boom box, her shiny silver whistle nearly touching the polished wood floor. When she stood up, the eight cheerleaders were all still frozen in place.

"I'm completely serious," she told them. "Practice is over." She walked off toward the door at the end of the gym, her immaculate white running shoes squeaking with every step and the ironed creases in her running suit as stiff as her indignation.

Melanie felt awful as she watched her go. The squad was tearing itself apart, and Melanie couldn't help believing that she was at least partly responsible.

"Way to go, Andrews," Vanessa said the moment Sandra disappeared. "Way to drag us *all* down."

"Shut up, Vanessa. Do the world a favor." Grabbing her gym bag from against the wall, Melanie trotted off after her coach.

She didn't follow Sandra to her office, though. Instead, she ran to her locker and got out her coat, pulling it on over her workout clothes. With her gym bag on one shoulder and her backpack on the other, she slammed her locker door and charged out of the gym, wanting to get clear of the place before Vanessa or any of the others followed. The way she was feeling, she didn't want to see any of them—not even Tanya or Angela. She just wanted to be alone.

But outside, a freezing rain had begun, pelting the icy ground and forcing her to stop and dig out her umbrella. *Great*, she thought, opening it under the covered walkway and peering out through the falling slush. The bus shelter was at the other corner of the school grounds—she'd never make it that far without getting soaked.

Just great. After the blazing exit she'd made, there was no way she was going back into the gym to ask one of the girls to drive her. Gathering her coat and belongings around her as closely as she could, she set off through the storm, her cheerleading shoes seeping ice water into her socks before she had even reached the access road. *Super.*

Melanie hurried as much as she dared on the slippery pavement. She almost wished Jesse would show up and whisk her away in his red BMW. Almost. There wasn't enough ice in the world to make her forget who the source of all this trouble was.

I never should have let him near me. I knew it was a bad idea.

Not that it had been all bad. There were times

when Jesse could be truly sweet. There were even times when she liked him a lot.

She just didn't love him. Every moment they spent together only made that more apparent. If she loved him, would she be irritated when he dropped by unexpectedly? Would she cringe every time he attempted to touch her in public? And now there was all this additional trouble on the squad—and after she had thought things couldn't get any worse!

I should probably break it off with him. Probably before I leave for California.

But that was only two days away now. It seemed awfully sudden. Was she even sure that was what she wanted?

She turned the corner from the access road onto the sidewalk along the main street. At last the bus stop was in sight. Jogging down half a block of icy sidewalk, she managed to keep her footing somehow until she was finally safe within its shelter. She dropped her bags onto a vacant bench and shook the water off her coat and umbrella.

She had a feeling Jesse would take a breakup hard.

But it's not even really a breakup—I certainly never made him any promises. It just didn't work out, that's all. I'd rather go back to the way things were.

Her mind was made up, she realized. She did want to end things now.

It'll be better this way. It will. And with me out of town for three days, he'll have a chance to see that too.

He won't be able to call or drop by. He might find out he doesn't even miss me.

The bus pulled up in a cloud of steam, and Melanie hurried to gather her things. Running up the steps into the heated bus, she dropped gratefully into the first empty seat.

Am I getting a swelled head or what? she laughed to herself, sinking down into the warmth. *Jesse miss me? By the time I get back from California, he'll probably already be working on his next victim.*

Fifteen

"Are we almost done?" Nicole complained from the backseat as her mother pulled into the shopping center parking lot Thursday evening. "I ought to have been home an hour ago, packing for my trip."

"I need to buy something for dinner," Mrs. Brewster replied, easing her car into a space beside the grocery store. "And maybe just a few other things, since we're here."

"Mom! This is my last night to pack! As far as I'm concerned, we can all skip dinner tonight."

"Speak for yourself," Heather said from in front. "Turning into a pipe cleaner isn't *everyone's* life ambition."

Nicole kicked the back of her sister's seat.

"Knock it off, you two. This is the last stop. You'll have plenty of time left to pack, Nicole."

Because of the nasty weather, Mrs. Brewster had picked both her daughters up from school that day. Unfortunately, conditions hadn't been ugly enough to send them straight home. Instead, Nicole had been forced to endure a string of boring errands when all she wanted to do was figure out how to stuff three or four more head-turning outfits into her already bulging suitcase.

"Can I wait in the car?" she asked as her mother turned off the ignition.

"No. I'm not leaving the heater running, and besides, I don't want you sitting out here in the parking lot like a dog. You'll come inside like any normal, *pleasant* human being."

"Fine," said Nicole, feeling anything but pleasant. The cloudy sky was dark now, and every minute she lost was killing her. She struck off across the parking lot at the fastest pace she could manage in her high-heeled boots, desperate to get the ordeal over with.

Inside the crowded store, it soon became apparent that her mom had no intention of buying only a few things. "Get a cart, Heather," she instructed. "I need to find my list." She began digging through her handbag while Heather retrieved a shopping cart.

"What?" Nicole wailed. "*What* list? And why do we need a cart if we're only buying a couple of things?"

Her mother fixed her with sharp blue eyes. "Stop acting like a two-year-old, Nicole, or I'll make you ride in it."

Nicole slouched sulkily down the aisle behind her and Heather as they pushed the cart through the store. It seemed as if Mrs. Brewster picked through the produce for an hour, and then the meat department met even greater scrutiny. Pasta, canned goods, cereal, dairy . . . Nicole could barely keep from screaming.

"All right," Mrs. Brewster finally announced. "We'll just get some paper towels and we're done."

"Hooray!" Nicole cheered sarcastically, earning another look from her mother.

Mrs. Brewster chose the economy pack of paper towels and set it on top of the groceries in their cart. "We might as well get some toilet paper, too."

Nicole's heart skipped at the sound of those words in her mother's mouth—especially there, at the scene of her crime. Still, it wasn't as if they didn't buy toilet paper nearly every trip. Heather picked up the package their mother pointed to and set it in the cart beside the paper towels without betraying the slightest emotion. *She's good*, Nicole thought grudgingly.

At the checkout stands, they finally caught a break. A new line opened right as they walked up. Grabbing the cart by its wire front, Nicole rushed it over to the open register and hurriedly began unloading items. The toilet paper first, then the paper towels. Next came the spaghetti sauce and—

"More toilet paper already?" an elderly voice asked. "My! What did you girls do with all the paper you bought here the other night?"

Nicole felt everything in her body freeze. Her heart had stopped—she was sure of that. Slowly, moving only the absolutely essential muscles, she looked up at the cashier.

The woman behind the register was the same gray-haired, granny-glasses-wearing checker she and Heather had used on the night of the big escapade. Nicole had been so intent on getting home that she had hustled into her line without even looking. And now she was trapped. She could feel her mother's too-blue eyes burning a hole through the back of her head.

"Maybe you have us confused with someone else," Heather suggested weakly.

The cashier drew back and cracked a big smile. "Like I'd forget you girls! Sisters for sure, that's what I told myself. Besides, it's not every day I sell twenty-four double rolls of toilet paper all by themselves. A sale like that kind of makes you take notice."

Nicole closed her eyes and wished herself in Siberia, or somewhere even farther away and harder to get to. *Thanks for helping, Heather.*

Her mother's voice, when it finally broke the ensuing silence, was one of the scariest things Nicole had ever heard. "Why don't you girls go wait in the car?"

An instant later, Nicole found herself in the icy air outside with almost no recollection of grabbing the car keys from her mother's hand or running out of the brightly lit store. She fumbled with the door lock, her fingers shaking so badly she couldn't get the key in. For once, Heather didn't offer advice. She stood shivering at Nicole's side, shock written all over her face.

173

"We are dead," she muttered over and over as Nicole fought with the door. "We are so dead."

The lock finally turned and the two of them tumbled into the backseat, neither one willing to risk the front. Nicole reached around to open the trunk from inside before she pulled the door shut behind them. Then, tossing the keys into the passenger seat, she checked through the window to make sure their mother hadn't left the store yet. As tempting as it was to go completely to pieces, she had to use her last minute wisely.

"Just don't forget our deal!" she threatened Heather. "It's not my fault we got caught, and I'm in as much trouble as you are. You'd better keep your lips zipped about anything else or you'll be really sorry."

"I'm already sorry," Heather moaned as their mom came out of the big glass door.

The two of them waited in silence while Mrs. Brewster unloaded her groceries into the open trunk, then slowly, slowly, let herself in on the driver's side. She picked the keys up off the passenger seat where Nicole had tossed them, started the engine, then peeled off her gloves.

"So," she said to the windshield, not turning her head an inch. "Do you girls have anything you want to say to me?"

"Am I still going to California?" Nicole blurted out, smacking a hand over her mouth in almost the same instant. It couldn't have been a more wrong thing to say.

Her mother turned around to stare at her in disbelief. "If it didn't involve disappointing Leah, I'd say 'absolutely not' right now. The only reason I'm going to talk to your father before I say no is that it's probably too late for her to replace you."

Mrs. Brewster put the car in gear and began backing out of the space. "I can tell you this, though: You won't need to waste any more time packing tonight."

The clock on her dad's dashboard read 9:45 when Leah pulled up in front of the del Rioses' house. Miguel's car was parked in its usual place under the streetlight. Leah edged into that puddle of light as well, then turned off the engine and sat indecisively.

I should have called before I came over, she thought. *Especially so late on a school night.* But Miguel had worked overtime again that Thursday afternoon, and tomorrow night she'd be on a plane to California. If she wanted to see him alone before she left, the time was now or never.

And we need some time together, she thought, climbing resolutely out of the car. *Or at least I do.* She didn't want to go off to California and leave things the strained way they'd been. As little as she'd seen him over the last few days, he was starting to feel like a stranger. Leah patted her coat pocket to make sure her list was inside, then began heading up the walkway.

Miguel opened the front door before she knocked, or she might still have chickened out.

"What are you doing here?" he whispered, stepping out onto his small front porch. "My mom and Rosa are asleep."

"How did you know I was out here?"

"I heard your car. What's up?"

His words were as clipped as the night air was cold. Leah wasn't sure which of those things had caused her to shiver. "Can I come in?" she asked.

Miguel shook his head. "Let's sit in your car. I don't want to wake anyone up."

This is getting off to a bad start, Leah thought as she turned and walked back the way she'd just come. *No hug, no invitation inside . . . he doesn't even look happy to see me*. She unlocked the passenger door for Miguel, then silently walked around and got in on the driver's side.

"I can't stay long," were the first words out of his mouth. "I've got that physiology quiz tomorrow and I have to study. I'm already going to be up until midnight."

"So why did you wait until the last minute?" Leah asked irritably.

"Because I had to work," Miguel replied, even more irritably.

I should have known the answer to that, Leah realized.

"Okay. Okay, look." She took her crumpled list out of her pocket and put it in his hands. "I didn't come here to fight with you. I wanted to show you this."

"What is it?' Miguel asked, fumbling for the dome

light on the ceiling of the car. He found the switch, and light flooded the small cabin.

" 'Ways to stay together'?" he said skeptically, reading from the top. "Where did this stuff come from?"

"What do you mean, where did it come from? From me. Those are my ideas."

Miguel's eyes skimmed down the list, barely glancing at the possibilities it had taken Leah hours to assemble. "I like number twelve."

"Miguel! That was a joke!"

Despite her earlier assumption that she could think of fifty ways to stay together, she had managed only eleven, and several of those were basically the same thing. Number twelve read: *Chuck everything. Forget about school. Move to Europe.*

"Well, what do you want me to say, Leah?"

"Don't you like any of the other choices?"

"I don't *see* any other choices. As far as I can tell, these are all you doing what you want and me working around it. You go to school, and I follow. You go on a modeling tour, and I follow. What about Clearwater University and my idea? You didn't even write that down."

"Because I don't want to go to that school and you know it! I don't even know how you could seriously suggest that."

"How about what you're suggesting? When I wanted to work right out of high school, you whined and whined about how I had to go to college. So now I've decided to go to college, and . . ." He paused to count. "*Five* of these ideas have me going straight to work. Why don't you just admit it, Leah? The only college education you really care about is yours."

"That's not true!"

"No? Try reading that list again."

Leah snatched it out of his hands and stuffed it back into her pocket. "It's easy to criticize, but I don't hear you coming up with anything."

"What do you expect me to do?"

"I expect you to do *something*. You're just letting this happen to us!"

"Nothing's happening yet."

"Exactly! Nothing's happening."

Miguel reached up again and switched off the overhead light. "Are we done? Because I've got to study."

Leah couldn't see well in the sudden darkness, but by the tone of his voice she could tell he was angry. That was okay—she was angry too now. "We're all done as far as I'm concerned."

"What's that supposed to mean?"

"Just that I'll see you at school tomorrow."

"Fine."

"Fine."

But it wasn't, and they both knew it.

Sixteen

"Well, I guess that's everything," Jenna said, zipping the last few items into her small suitcase. "Wow, I can't believe I'm really going!" It seemed like only yesterday that Leah had called to invite her to California, and in just a few hours she'd be on a plane.

She set the suitcase with her backpack by her bedroom door, then did one last slow circuit of her room to make sure she wasn't forgetting something important. She'd packed two pairs of jeans, two pairs of shorts, and a pair of dress pants, as well as three casual tops, one silk blouse, a bathing suit, and all the usual shoes, socks, et cetera. She'd wear both her coat and blazer on the plane, to save having to pack them. As far as she could tell, she hadn't forgotten a thing.

Except that she had hoped Caitlin was going to get home in time to say good-bye.

Jenna glanced at the clock on her desk. Leah and her parents were due to arrive any minute to pick her up for the trip to the St. Louis airport. If Caitlin had been able to get off work early, she should have been home before now.

"I guess I'll have to leave her a note."

Using a Post-it from her desk, Jenna scribbled a quick good-bye. There was a book on the ledge behind Caitlin's bed, and Jenna pressed her note to the cover. As she did, she noticed the edge of a white envelope peeking out from between the pages.

David's envelope, she thought instantly, glancing guiltily toward the open doorway. She remembered seeing Caitlin destroy the letter, but not the envelope. Carefully, so as not to lose Caitlin's place, Jenna pulled the envelope out halfway, curious to see it again. It wasn't the envelope she'd expected.

What's this? The white rectangle was addressed in Caitlin's neat handwriting—to David!

She hasn't given him Mary Beth's address yet! A week had passed since Caitlin had received his letter asking for it and—while Jenna hadn't dared to bring up the subject since that tearful afternoon—she'd assumed that Caitlin had answered right away. Unless this was some *other* letter . . . maybe one Caitlin was embarrassed to send . . .

"That's it. I'm calling Peter," Jenna said, already reaching for the phone. It was ridiculous to keep quiet any longer when together the two of them might still be able to fix the whole thing. A moment later, he was on the line and she launched headlong into the story.

180

"Peter? Hi, it's me. Did you know that David wrote Caitlin and asked for Mary Beth's address? Because—"

"Did he? I wondered if he was going to."

"What?" gasped Jenna. "Why?"

"He told me the morning he left that he might."

"He *told* you? Why didn't you tell me?"

"What for?" Peter said, clearly unaware of the importance of that information. "Hey, when are you leaving? I thought you were already gone."

"Peter! Don't you know what you've done? *Caitlin* likes David."

There was a silence on the other end. "I . . . That's a surprise," he said finally. "But I'm not exactly sure how *I* did that."

"Not *that*! You knew he liked Mary Beth, and you didn't do anything."

"Huh? I don't know if he likes Mary Beth—maybe he just wants to write her a letter. And besides, what did you expect me to do?"

"Well, you could have at least told me."

"You mean the way you told me about Caitlin?"

Jenna walked to the lilac-draped window and stared blindly at the gathering darkness outside, completely frustrated. She was going to have to leave any second, and they were wasting valuable time.

"I *couldn't* tell you about Caitlin," she said, trying to keep her voice calm, "because she swore me to secrecy."

"Oh." For a moment he finally seemed to get it.

"So why doesn't she care that you're telling me now?"

"Are you kidding? Of course she cares! It's just that I don't think she's written David back yet, and I was hoping there was some way that you and I could . . . I don't know. I want to help her."

"Do you want me to send David an e-mail? I can tell him Caitlin's interested and find out if he is too."

"No!" Jenna said immediately. "You can't tell him that! If Caitlin ever found out, she'd never trust me again."

"Why did you tell me, then?" Peter sounded a little annoyed. "If I'm not supposed to know, and I'm not supposed to tell, I'd just as soon never have heard about it."

"Strangely enough, I thought you *might* know who your own brother likes," Jenna said. "But since you don't, you could find out without mentioning Caitlin, couldn't you? And if it's Mary Beth, you could steer him away from her."

"What have you got against Mary Beth?"

"Nothing! It's just . . . she'll find someone else. Caitlin won't."

"I'm not going to tell my brother who to like," Peter said stubbornly. "That's David's business, and I think we ought to stay out of it."

"Okay, so we'll stay out of it! Just try to find out, all right?"

"I'll see. If it comes up."

Jenna wanted to tell him to *make* it come up, but he was already sounding testy and she didn't want to start a fight. "All right. I'd better go because Leah's going to be here any minute. Will you miss me?"

"You know I will."

"Yeah. I'll miss you too."

"Have fun. And bring me back a Fire & Water T-shirt!"

"I will. Bye."

Jenna clicked off the cordless phone, turning away from the window to put it back on the nightstand. But the sight that caught her eyes as she did stopped her in midmotion, contracting her stomach into a hard little knot.

Caitlin was standing just inside the doorway, tears streaming from her eyes.

"Caitlin!" Jenna cried. "How, uh . . . I mean, when . . . ?"

Caitlin's only answer was a horrible, accusing look before she ran out of their room, pounding down the stairs to the second floor.

She heard everything, Jenna realized. *Or enough of it, anyway.*

The door of the second-floor bathroom slammed.

Sick with remorse, Jenna hurried down the stairs and knocked on the bathroom door. "Caitlin? Caitlin, let me in. I can explain."

There was no sound from the bathroom, but the doorbell rang downstairs.

"Jenna!" Mrs. Conrad called. "The Rosenthals are here."

"Coming!" Jenna shouted, then turned back to the door. "Caitlin, please. Let me in, all right?"

Still no answer. Taking a deep breath, Jenna tried the doorknob. Locked.

"Jenna!" her mother called again. "You have a plane to catch!"

"Cat, please just open the door," Jenna begged. "At least let me say I'm sorry."

But Caitlin refused to acknowledge her presence, and in the end Jenna had to run for her suitcase and leave, her guilt weighing more than her luggage.

"Good. She's still here!" Jesse said with relief, pulling into the Andrewses' driveway.

Melanie was standing on her front doorstep, a suitcase and a small cardboard box at her feet, and even though the sky was more than half dark, her red coat stood out clearly against the white door. His heart turned over at the sight. She was so beautiful, so small and perfect. . . .

"You're late," she said as he slammed his car door and trotted up to meet her.

"I know. I'm sorry. My dad came home from work right as I was leaving, with all kinds of stupid stuff for me to do. I got here as soon as I could."

Melanie frowned. "Well, there's no time now."

"No time for what?"

"For what I had in mind."

"Really?" Jesse pulled her into his arms, intrigued. "Is there enough time for this?" he asked playfully, lowering his lips to hers.

"No. There isn't." Melanie's hands found his stomach, and her stiff arms pushed him away. "There's *especially* not time for that."

"Why not?" he asked. Had he come on too strong? Melanie was so hard to judge. Usually she responded to confidence, but there were times when she seemed to want something completely different. And he still hadn't figured out what.

"You and I . . . ," she began, her eyes sad and distant. "Jesse, this just isn't working out. That's why I wanted you to come over this afternoon. I wanted to tell you that."

"What?"

"We tried, but . . . I don't think it's meant to be. It just doesn't feel right."

"Says who? Do I get a vote?"

Melanie shook her head. "I'm sorry, Jesse. My mind's made up."

"But, Melanie, I don't understand! Weren't things going pretty well? I mean, I know they weren't perfect, but give us a chance! We'll get better, I swear."

"No. It's better to end it now, before anyone gets hurt."

Jesse stared, unable to believe his ears. Did she honestly believe that ending it now wouldn't hurt him? And what about her? Was she saying she didn't feel *anything* for him? He couldn't accept that—not after the last few days.

"We need to talk about this," he said. "If you tell me what you think is wrong, maybe I can fix it."

She only shook her head again, her blond hair swinging under a crushed felt hat. "I don't think so. It's hard to explain, but I guess . . . I'm just looking for something that's real in my life. Do you understand? Just one real thing. And you . . . can't give me that."

She stooped down and picked up the box at her feet, putting it into his hands. "Here, you should have this back. It doesn't belong to me."

He knew without looking that it was his angel figurine.

"You're making a big mistake," he pleaded, just as a sweep of headlights illuminated the driveway. A Ford pulled in behind his BMW, cutting its lights to keep from blinding them.

Melanie waved at the car and lifted her suitcase off the doorstep. "I don't think so. Think about it this weekend, and you're going to see that I'm right."

Then, before he could argue, or kiss her good-bye, or even carry her bag, she was off, tossing her suitcase into the trunk and climbing into the backseat.

"Hi, Jesse!" Jenna called to him through the open car door. The hand waving from the passenger seat was Leah's.

But Melanie didn't wave. She didn't even look at

him as the car backed up and turned around on the private road. A moment later, she was gone: nothing but two taillights, then darkness.

It was over.

Jesse wandered down to the place where the Ford had been, unable to believe what had just happened. If she was so unhappy with him, how could he not have known it? How come he hadn't seen this coming?

Then he looked down at the box in his hands and felt a sudden rush of anger. He'd taken a lot of risks for Melanie. He'd shown her parts of himself that other girls had only begged to see: real emotion, real affection. There *had* been something real between them—how could she say there hadn't?

He wanted to hurl the porcelain angel against her door and leave it there in shards.

"Would that be real enough for her?" he wondered bitterly. Reaching into the box, he snatched the delicate sculpture from its nest of protective paper, cocking his right arm to fire off a blazing forward pass.

But something held him back. He tried again, hesitated again. He had so little left from his mother . . . In the end he dropped the figure into the box, tossed it into his BMW, and hurriedly climbed in behind it.

She's not worth it, he thought, backing out of the Andrewses' driveway. The smell of burned rubber stung his nostrils as he wheeled his car through a three-sixty at the end of her street and shot forward into the darkness.

Sooner or later, she's going to realize that breaking up with me was the biggest mistake of her life. No one else will ever want her more than I did. I would have given her anything. Anything!

He swiped distractedly at something trickling down the side of his nose and found out his whole face was wet. The discovery that he was crying only made him angrier.

That day is coming, I swear. And when it does, she can beg all she wants to. I'm finished with Melanie Andrews!

"Hurry, hurry, hurry," Nicole urged herself under her breath. The added pressure only made her that much crazier. She bounced from her closet to her dresser to the bathroom, unable to remember what it was she had wanted to add to her second suitcase.

Her parents had made her wait an hour after she got home from school that Friday before Mrs. Brewster had finally announced their decision: Nicole could still go to California, but only because it was too late to cancel on the Rosenthals. She'd be grounded for two weeks when she got back.

Nicole had leapt off the couch, thrown her arms around her surprised mother, then flown up the stairs to pack an additional bag. Being grounded had never sounded so good, so completely fair and reasonable. Nicole didn't care if they kept her locked up for two months, as long as she went to California first.

Heather, whose imprisonment had already started, was less thrilled about the verdict.

"It's not fair," she complained for the fifteenth time, barging through their bathroom. "You're going to California, and I'm not even allowed to make a phone call. And it's a three-day weekend, too!"

"Your problem," Nicole said unsympathetically. Where did she put her red headband? "TP'ing that house was your brilliant idea, don't forget."

"Yeah, well, if Mom knew what you had *really* done—"

Hair accessories were completely forgotten as Nicole dashed across the room and grabbed Heather by the shirt. "We had a deal," she whispered, staring deep into Heather's eyes. "If you're even *thinking* about ratting me out now—"

"Save your threats," Heather said, twisting out of Nicole's grasp. "I hope you have a lousy time." She turned and walked back through the bathroom to her bedroom, slamming the door shut behind her.

"Good riddance, creep," Nicole muttered, resuming her last-minute packing. Leah would be there any second.

If only Courtney were coming! Her best friend hadn't spoken to her since their fight on Tuesday, clearly hoping that more of the silent treatment would change Nicole's mind. Nicole's hand drifted toward the phone lying on the bed beside her suitcase. *Maybe I should call to say good-bye*, she thought. *I could ask her what she wants for a souvenir.*

A moment later she abandoned the idea. *Knowing Court, that'll only make her madder.*

No, Courtney would have to wait. Once the trip was over, Nicole was sure she could smooth things over somehow. *Pretty sure, anyway.*

She took a deep breath to clear her mind, then returned to the job at hand. Her new Christmas suitcase was already closed and standing by her bedroom door. She tossed a few last essentials into her smaller second bag, then decided to take them both down to the front door to join her carry-on stuff.

As she lugged her heavy load down the stairs, it occurred to her once again that she must be destined to go on this trip. First the unexpected invitation, then the unexpected gift of a new suitcase, then the unexpected reprieve from certain TP disaster . . .

She'd asked for a sign, and she'd gotten three.

A car horn suddenly blared in the driveway. To Nicole it just sounded like sweet confirmation.

Seventeen

"Are you going to be okay here, sweetheart?" Mrs. Rosenthal asked worriedly at the boarding gate. "I'd like to see your plane take off, but I really don't know about that place I parked the car—I think they might actually tow me there. With all the luggage we needed to carry, though . . ." Her mother just barely glanced at Nicole, but Leah knew exactly what she meant.

"I'll be fine. If you've seen one plane take off, you've seen them all." She wrapped her mother in a fierce hug, suddenly wishing Mrs. Rosenthal would forget her work commitments and come after all, knowing it was too late to say so. "I'll call you and tell you what happens," she whispered huskily.

Her mom rubbed her back. "I hope you win, if that's what you want. Just remember, your father and I couldn't be more proud of you either way."

Leah felt tears rush up behind her lashes, and the last thing she wanted was to cry in such a big crowd. Melanie, Nicole, and Jenna were standing beside them at the windows looking over the runway, and at least a hundred other people packed the area around the gate in preparation for boarding the sold-out flight. With a nod, Leah stepped out of her mother's embrace. "I'll keep you posted."

"Okay. Are you sure you're all right?"

"Of course. Tell Dad I love him." There hadn't been room for both her parents in the car besides four girls and their luggage—that had been decided even before anyone knew how much stuff Nicole was going to bring: two large suitcases, three tote-style carry-ons, a huge makeup case, and a bunch of other, loose items, which the girls had had to divide up among them to meet the luggage restrictions.

Mrs. Rosenthal nodded. "I'm going, then. Be sure to call."

Leah nodded mutely, the lump in her throat making speech impossible.

"Good-bye, girls. Have a nice trip," Mrs. Rosenthal said, waving as she walked off. "I'll pick you up here Tuesday."

"Bye! Thank you!" Nicole shouted, waving frantically.

Jenna and Melanie smiled and waved silently.

Leah was so used to Melanie's silences that her failure to say much on the long drive from Clearwater Crossing to St. Louis hadn't seemed remarkable. For Jenna to be so subdued, however, was definitely out of character. Leah wondered if her friend was already missing Peter, or if something else was wrong.

Not that anyone else could get a word in the way Nicole was yakking. At least someone is glad to be going.

Leah watched her mother disappear into the crowd that pulsed through the terminal. Everywhere people with suitcases, laptops, briefcases, backpacks, and babies pushed and were pushed on the way to their destinations. And there were couples, too: guys with their arms around their girls' waists, girls hugging their boyfriends' necks. The sight made her long for Miguel.

They had eaten lunch together at school that day and said their good-byes then. Because he was working again that night, he hadn't been able to come see her off. She wondered what he was doing at that moment, and if he was thinking of her. . . .

"Flight 384 for Los Angeles is now available for preboarding," a woman's voice said over a speaker. "If you are a first-class passenger, if you are traveling with small children, or if you require extra time getting down the gangway, you may board the aircraft at this time."

"That's us!" Nicole said excitedly. "Do you think we should get in line?"

"No," said Leah. "They mean people with disabilities, not extra luggage. Wait until they call the rows we're sitting in."

"We could get ready to move when they call us, though," Melanie suggested, throwing a significant glance at the disorganized pile of totes, water bottles, magazines, snacks, and travel games by Nicole's feet.

Jenna bent down and listlessly picked up the tote holding Nicole's Discman and CDs. Her own backpack was already on her shoulders.

"At this time, we would like to begin general boarding from the rear of the aircraft," the amplified voice announced. Row numbers were mentioned, and more people started moving toward the gate.

"Oh, this is so exciting!" Nicole squealed.

Melanie smiled faintly.

Even though their row hadn't yet been called, the four girls managed to gather up all Nicole's stuff and started wandering toward the gate. Night had long since fallen outside. Through the windows, Leah could see the lit-up nose of the plane they would board, and the string of runway lights behind it. The sky was cold but clear, and each light was as sharp as glass.

"Leah! Leah, wait!" a deep voice rang out behind her, cutting cleanly through the other noise in the terminal.

"Miguel?" She turned around disbelievingly, looking for him in the crowd. "Miguel!"

He was running toward her through the mob, a bouquet clutched in one hand. "Leah, wait!"

Leah dropped Nicole's makeup case on the floor, along with two magazines, a neck pillow, and a paperback. Shrugging off her own backpack, she ran to meet him halfway.

"You came!" she cried, throwing herself into his arms. She couldn't have cared less that he was still dressed in paint-spattered work jeans, or that she was crushing the roses he'd brought her. All she wanted to do was hold him, be safe in his arms, and feel the incredible joy of knowing that he still loved her enough to leave work and drive all the way to St. Louis just to say good-bye.

"I can't believe you're really here," she said, stepping back and wiping away happy tears.

"I know. Me either." His handsome face showed his emotion as he put the flowers into her hands. "I just couldn't let you go off like this . . . not with everything so messed up between us. I wouldn't have slept for four nights."

Leah laughed through her tears. "I *haven't* slept for four nights. Oh, Miguel, I love you so much."

She started to hug him again, but he stopped her, holding her at arm's length with strong hands on her waist.

"I thought of a way we can stay together," he told her, searching her eyes. "A *good* way. One that would make us both happy."

"Really?" she said hopefully. "I thought I'd thought of everything."

Miguel shook his head. "I don't think you thought of this."

And there was something in his gaze that made her suddenly weak on her feet.

Fumbling in his front jeans pocket, he pulled out a plain silver ring, one she had seen him wear on occasion, and held it up in front of him.

"I didn't know I was going to do this until just before I left," he explained. "I didn't have much time to prepare. . . ."

Then, as Leah watched transfixed, he went down on one knee in front of all those people.

"I love you, Leah Rosenthal. Will you marry me?"

How Real Are You?

Your answers to the following quiz
will clue you in!

How Real Are You?

Being true to yourself isn't always easy. Remembering who you are and what you believe can be a real balancing act when you also have to consider the pressures and expectations of family, friends, and even total strangers. When you're faced with a tough situation, do you react based on your true convictions? Or do you make decisions that reflect the desires and demands of the moment? Take our special quiz to find out how real *you* are.

1. *A friend apologizes for not showing up to meet you at the mall on Saturday but says her parents kept her home all weekend. She obviously doesn't know you saw her going into Burger City with Brian Dawson later that same afternoon. You:*
   A. Overlook her lie—who *wouldn't* rather go out with Brian?
   B. Confront her with the facts.
   C. Say nothing but start looking for a more honest friend.

2. *Ethan Ryan is your absolute favorite movie star. You're about to leave for the premiere of his long-awaited new film when a friend calls you up in tears, begging for advice on her latest problem. You:*
   A. Invite her to come to the movie with you.

B. Cancel the premiere and talk for an hour.

C. Tell her you'll call her tomorrow.

3. A popular girl at your school has always been nasty to you. When you hear an embarrassing rumor about her, you:

A. Rush to tell everyone. Payback time!

B. Tell only your best friend.

C. Do your best to forget you ever heard it.

4. At church you are friendly with Matt, but at school everyone thinks he's a geek. When he unexpectedly asks you to the prom, you:

A. Go. If you don't, he'll think you're stuck up.

B. Go. Who cares what other people think?

C. Thank him but say you don't like him that way.

5. A friend asks for your honest opinion of her new outfit. You think it looks like a cross between a garage sale and a costume party, but you don't want to hurt her feelings. You:

A. Tell the truth as gently as possible.

B. Tell a white lie. After all, it's only clothes.

C. Find a way to change the subject.

6. You and some friends are on your way into a restaurant when a homeless man asks you for money. You:

A. Give him a dollar.

B. Say you don't have any change.

C. Get all your friends to pitch in and buy him a meal instead.

7. *Some of your friends from church are meeting to pray at the school flagpole. You:*
   A. Join them.
   B. Invite everyone you know.
   C. Skip it. How embarrassing!

8. *You are with a group of friends at the music store when one of them slips a CD into her purse. She's never done anything like that before, and you seem to be the only person who saw it. You:*
   A. Tell her to put it back but don't make a scene when she doesn't.
   B. Do nothing, then lie awake at night feeling guilty.
   C. Report her to a store employee.

9. *The guy of your dreams has finally asked you out. You're thrilled! But when you wake up on the morning of the big event, there's an enormous red zit on the end of your nose. You:*
   A. Call and tell him you're sick.
   B. Go anyway—your skin isn't who you are.
   C. Go but wear industrial-strength makeup.

10. *You've heard the Bible verse "Honor your father and your mother" a thousand times, but your parents are*

dead set against underage drinking and you know there's going to be a keg at a party you're invited to. Everyone who matters will be there—if you don't show up you'll look like a social outcast. You:

A. Go to the party and don't tell your folks about the beer.

B. Tell them, then get angry when they forbid you to go. Don't they trust you?

C. Thank the person who invited you but say you attend only alcohol-free events.

Scoring

1. A—0, B—2, C—1
2. A—1, B—0, C—2
3. A—0, B—1, C—2
4. A—0, B—2, C—1
5. A—2, B—0, C—1
6. A—1, B—0, C—2
7. A—1, B—2, C—0
8. A—1, B—0, C—2
9. A—0, B—2, C—1
10. A—0, B—1, C—2

If your score is 0 to 6:

What other people think matters to you a *lot*. If that's part of who you really are, fine. But if you're avoiding things you ought to be dealing with, or making decisions based on what you fear other people will think, maybe it's time to reconsider. Also, there might be times when a little more reflection would result in a kinder approach. If you establish your own core set of values and priorities, tough situations will be easier to deal with in a real and meaningful way.

If your score is 7 to 13:

You're secure in who you are, but you don't live in a vacuum, either. You know what matters to you, and you're also willing to make allowances for others. This middle-of-the-road approach will not only serve you well, people will appreciate you for it. Just make sure you don't compromise on the things that really matter. Know when to cut yourself some slack or bend for a friend—and know when to stand your ground.

If your score is 14 to 20:

You are extremely honest, both with yourself and with others, and not afraid to stand up for what you believe in. People may not always appreciate your hard-line approach, but eventually they'll respect you for it. Just be sure that the standards you set for yourself are always at least as high as the standards you set for others, and don't become so set in your opinions that you close your mind. Flexibility *can* be a virtue.